Deadly
Misconduct

R.J. Amos

For Mum, who has read this book more times than it deserved and told me each time that it was just because she enjoyed it.

I was determined to enjoy myself at the conference dinner that Thursday night even though I'd usually prefer to be tucked up at home with a nice glass of wine and a good book. This was my chance to catch up properly with my conference buddies, Robbie and Misaki. We had worked together at various universities and now we only managed to visit at conferences. There was always a lot to catch up on. And never quite enough time to do it.

Misaki and I had met in Adelaide where I was on my first post-doctoral position and she was a fresh-faced PhD student. We had cubicles next to each other in the office and often worked on the same lab bench. I used to help her bring better English into her writing and she would bring back treats from home that were different from anything I had ever tasted, and sometimes even yummy. And always good for a laugh. I laughed at her for eating the stuff, and she at me for being so tame in my tastes. One day we are going to head to Japan together and I'm going to eat such delicacies as hot chocolate in a can from a vending machine, and a special dish she's told me about where the fish is sliced so thinly that it waves in the hot air rising from the dish and looks like it's still alive. I'm not sure why anyone would want to eat anything that still looks alive, but I'll eat it if she asks me to. And if there's lots of sake.

Robbie was (and still is) the lab manager of the lab where I worked in Sydney. He is a totally ocker Aussie bloke and pretty blunt in what he says and how he says it. But I think that somewhere inside him there is a heart of gold. I'm not really sure why we're friends, to be honest, maybe he says things that I wish I could, but don't, because I'm such a good girl. Or maybe it's the way he looked after me when I first arrived in Sydney, and made sure I was settled and happy working in his lab. Maybe he puts up with me because I listen to what he has to say without arguing, well, without arguing too much. We're not exactly an obvious pairing, still, it's a friendship that's lasted and it was good to be able to catch up again.

So there we were, the three of us, catching up again after a long break, and able to chat about everyday things after a long week of scientific lectures and poster presentations.

The conference that had brought my friends to me was held in Hobart, Tasmania (known as Tassie to the locals). Which was really handy, because I lived in Kingston Beach, Tasmania, about 10 minutes away by car and I didn't need to catch planes or stay in hotels or do any of that expensive stuff. You see, I was attending this conference in the hope of finding a job, a research position at a university. I was qualified and experienced and had worked for about ten years as a researcher and lecturer. But then my mother got ill and I came home to care for her. Dropped everything. Nothing else was important, not when Mum needed me. And she really needed me. And I was so glad that I was home with her for those last few months, and then I needed the time to recover – to walk on the beach, to write in my journal, to cry, to think, to wander around in an unseeing haze for a while.

Then one day I woke up and realised that I needed to go back to work. I needed to start thinking about supporting myself. I needed to find a professor who would take me on after my long break from research, from publishing my chemistry. Too long a break in your publications and you're toast – no chance of getting funding, no chance of moving up the ladder. No matter whether I felt like it or not, I needed to get moving again.

But without a job, without a source of funding and a university to be attached to, attending academic conferences, making connections, and finding professors to talk to was just a little difficult. I could write emails, but I knew that professors get them every week from every Tom, Dick, and Harry. How could I bring my shining personality to the table without a table to talk at? I needed a way to display my wares, to convince someone to take me on.

And then this conference had fallen into my lap. I had started my job search by heading to the local uni and asking them if there was any work available, just on the off-chance. There wasn't anything, as I had thought, it was really the wrong time of year to be asking when you think about funding schedules and such, but my old honours supervisor had wangled me a ticket to the conference out of the goodness of her heart. I had a week to make a good impression.

I had made good use of the time. Professor Conneally, from Cambridge, had given a brilliant talk on the first day of the conference and I had made sure I talked to him about it, not straight afterwards, but later in the conference. And he had made noises about inviting me to his group. He had some funding coming, he said, and he was sure that he could make room for me. His group was biochemistry but he was a far-seeing bloke and was willing to take a chance that collaboration with a chemist like me could add value to the work he was doing. We were going to have a longer talk about it on Friday and line it all up.

But before that came the conference dinner. It was a chance for some good food, reasonably good wine, and for us all to let down our hair after all the lectures and deep thinking of the previous few days. Hobart had come to the party too with mild, even warm, weather (by Tasmanian standards). The restaurant chosen for the dinner looked out over the Derwent River and the decorations inside the spacious room were complemented by the sight of ferries passing by filled with their own evening parties, and even the occasional yacht motoring back to its mooring.

The fluid conversation rose and swelled around the room with occasional fountains of laughter bubbling over. All the delegates were chilling out, eating, drinking, and swapping stories of previous conference dinners, interesting lab accidents, bush walks, fun student behaviour, just about anything. Well, almost all of the delegates – Misaki, Robbie, and I passed the time waiting to be served by making a study of the different behaviours on show at the head table where the keynote lecturers were seated.

The table held eight people, all of them either the big stars of the conference, or the plus-one belonging to the big star. On one end was Professor Conneally – tall, fit, stylish, with his wife sitting next to him. Next to the Conneallys was Professor Anne Starly from the United States, followed by Professor Yuri Ostanov and his wife, then Professor Izumi Ali and finally Professor Brasindon and his wife right on the other end. We had learned earlier in the conference that Professor Conneally and Professor Brasindon had started their research careers together here in Australia but there may have been a good reason to separate them on the VIP table. They had very different takes on life. While Prof Conneally was enjoying the dinner and the atmosphere, Brasindon was still completely focussed on the research.

'Does Professor Brasindon ever stop working?' Misaki asked, 'I think he is even writing notes on the table napkins.'

'It's a good thing they're paper.' I said, folding mine in half and sticking it into my fork.

'Conneally is the complete opposite – holding court with all the gorgeous girls,' Robbie put in. 'Not judging – I know which end of the table I'd like to be on.'

'Yes, me too, the fun end,' I said.

'Dr Alicia Conway,' Robbie mocked me, 'I was sure you'd say Brasindon's end. You're so shallow.'

Not that I wanted to be surrounded by gorgeous girls, but there were loud shrieks of laughter and endless giggles coming from that end of the table. It made me wonder a bit what the research group was actually like and whether I'd fit in. The younger crowd were gravitating to the fun, and the crowd at that table was predominantly girls, leaving all the male delegates to their beer and wine at the lesser tables. The professor was attractive, there was no denying it, and yet his wife sitting next to him was the dumpy type – short, round, wearing a pastel pink cardigan, greying hair. She stood out negatively next to the bevy of beauties trying to get Conneally's attention.

There was the girl that Robbie introduced to me on the first day of the conference – Lisa – dressed fit to kill. She always looked like something out of a magazine, but there was more cleavage involved tonight and a shorter skirt, and she must have spent hours on her makeup – there was sparkley stuff around her eyes, and her face was, you know, made up. I don't know how to describe it and I don't know how it's done – you can tell I'm not the dressy type. Despite this being a dinner I was wearing jeans and a shirt like always. A nice shirt in honour of the dinner but I preferred to have pre-dinner drinks with my friends than spend that time troweling makeup on.

There was that other girl, the one I think of as 'headphones girl' because I saw her in one of the conference sessions watching a movie on her laptop and wearing headphones. Yes, headphones, covering both ears. You'd think she'd at least pretend that she wanted to be at the conference but there was no hiding her boredom that day. Today, on the other hand, she looked absolutely fascinated with whatever the professor was saying. I wondered whether something had changed or whether she was putting it on in the interests of getting a position working with Conneally's group. Or whether the conversation around Conneally was just so much fun that she didn't have to pretend to be interested.

'Did I just see her drop something into Conneally's bag? How weird.'

'What?' said Robbie.

'I'm sure I saw that girl put something into the bag next to Conneally's seat.' I edged my seat out and looked up the aisle between the tables.

'How could you see that from this angle?' Robbie also craned his back to see what he could see up at the top table.

The conversation degenerated into a good-natured argument about who could see what from what angle. That was our friendship really, arguments about things that didn't really matter.

'If you sat over here, you could see that the end of the table is in clear view.' I leant over slightly to make my point.

'Look whatever, but she's standing right in front of the bag. There's no way that you could see her do anything.' Robbie waved at the girl, who had obviously changed her position now.

'You have no idea, you're not taking into account the movement of the people around the table.' And so on.

Misaki listened for a while and then got bored. That also happened a lot around our friendship.

'I'm so hungry, I wonder what's on the menu,' she picked up the decorated card from the middle of the table and read from it, 'Starters: savoury quiches. We've had that. Mains:

beef and chicken (alternate drop), Dessert: cheesecake and lemon tart (alternate drop). If I get the beef can I swap with someone for the chicken?'

'I'll swap,' I said. Sometimes on nights like this I wish I had a husband so that we could swap meals or share desserts. But I have to admit it would be rather extreme to get married just to be able to swap a meal on the occasional night out. And friends like Misaki made the swapping possible anyway.

'I wonder if there's a Murphy's law for eating – you know, something about how service always starts at the other end of the room.' I drummed my fingers on the table.

'The speed of service is inversely proportional to the hunger of the people sitting at the table,' said Robbie.

'That would be it.'

'If you're going to be like that,' said Misaki, 'you need to go up to the special table and write chemical equations on napkins like Brasindon and company.'

We looked up to the table again. They were being served now, and I recognised one of the servers from somewhere, a blonde girl in her late twenties, but this was Tasmania – everyone knows everyone in Tasmania. She could be my second-cousin or some such relative who I hadn't seen for years, or someone I hung out at the beach with at some stage. I was trying to remember where I might know her from when something happened that put all that out of my mind.

Professor Conneally stopped talking, grabbed his chest and started to gasp. His wife turned to him, stretching out her hand, but he shook her off and stood up to move away from the table. His chair fell over behind him and he fell on top of it.

Robbie responded immediately, his first aid training taking over. He stood up and ran to the top table, along with a few other diners. The bevy of beauties that had been so attentive was pushed aside and their giggles turned to panicked shrieks.

I lost sight of Robbie and the head table as the news of Conneally's collapse spread like wild fire, and diners began to stand up, crowding around, trying to see the action. Mrs Conneally was screaming and sobbing. The wait staff ran in from every direction.

'Does he have pills? Conneally, do you have pills to take?'

'Is he choking?'

'Is it a stroke? I know what to do with a stroke.'

'It's a heart attack. I'm sure it's a heart attack.'

'Someone call an ambulance!'

It was all so completely unexpected. So totally out of the blue. I collapsed back into my chair and my mind slowed down and refused to process what was going on. I found myself begging the ambulance to hurry up, wishing these amateurs would stop mucking around, wishing that someone with some authority could calm the situation. I knew how much relief there had been during my mother's illness when the visiting nurse would come and take over and I could relax in knowing the right treatment was being dispensed. How much more in this emergency situation did we need someone who knew the drill, who could fix things, make it all right. Where was the ambulance? How long did it take to get here?

How long can panic last for?

Eventually the sounds of sirens cut through the uproar of the restaurant. The officers in their bright yellow assessed the situation and lifted the prostrate body onto a stretcher and moved him to the ambulance, and the wait staff calmed the diners and continued to serve the plates of food. Robbie left with the ambulance officers, as did Mrs Conneally. The Conneally's table settings were removed and the restaurant management tried to make it look as if nothing had happened.

But I couldn't pretend nothing had happened. I was stunned, I felt like I couldn't breathe. The grief that I had thought I was getting over rose and swirled around my head like a thick fog. Through the fog came scraps of conversation, 'what do you think happened?' 'heart attack?' 'do you think he'll be alright?' but I couldn't respond. I was too busy trying to hold myself together.

I felt a gentle hand on my arm, 'Are you ok?' asked Misaki. That was all it took, the tears welled and dripped down my face and I ran outside with Misaki following. Not that outside was much better. The ambulance was still there with its back doors open and paramedics in high-vis clothing were milling around.

I sank down on the footpath, resting my back against the cool restaurant wall. I felt nauseous and faint. But I thought Misaki needed an explanation so through my tears I told of my mother's death from pancreatic cancer just a few short months ago and the grief that had been resurrected by the scene in the restaurant.

'Is that why we didn't hear from you for all that time? I'm so sorry.' Misaki put her arm around my shoulders.

'I'll be ok, I just need to be alone for a while. Thanks for caring for me – but you go ahead and enjoy the meal. I just don't think I can eat now.'

'Will you get home ok?'

'I'm sure I'll be fine. Thanks so much, but I'm ok.' I just wanted to be left alone. Just for a while.

Misaki checked a few more times then headed back into the restaurant to finish her interrupted dinner.

I sat for a bit longer, the cool air and the sound of water lapping against the wharf wall helping me to calm down.

After what felt like a long time Robbie appeared from the direction of the ambulance. He sank to the ground and put his head in his hands. I sat down beside him. I had never seen him like this.

'Will he be alright?' I asked.

He shook his head, 'They tell me there was nothing I could have done. I don't know, I don't know.'

'But ...'

'Don't talk to me. Just ...'

'Right'

We sat together for a while and watched the ambulance doors close on the covered stretcher. Mrs Conneally, weeping copiously, was helped into a car and driven away. The footpath emptied of people, the show was over.

Eventually, I became aware of the hard ground, and the hard wall. I creaked and groaned and pulled myself up and brushed myself off, and Robbie joined me.

'What are you going to do?' I asked.

'Go back to the hotel and destroy the mini bar.'

'Right,' there wasn't much to say to that.

'You?'

'Home. Bed. Probably lie awake all night, processing.'

'Right. Each to his own.'

'Look after yourself, Robbie. Don't do anything stupid.'

'Don't worry about me. You take care.'

'Alright.'

We wandered into the night, each wrapped in our personal bubble of pain.

I slept, eventually, and I slept in. Woke up to sunshine and a much clearer head. Oh boy, the shock from experiencing the death up close was intense, and it showed me I had so much more grief to work through. What kind of stupid person even begins to think that they can be 'normal' in half a year or so after their mother dies. I'm wondering now whether 'normal' is even an option.

Anyway, once I woke up I headed to The Lemon Tree for coffee and comfort. Jan, the owner, looks after me. It makes a difference when you've known someone since primary school. She knows what I need to get through.

I remember when I first turned up at primary school, starting a new school in grade two because Mum and I had just moved into the area. I was wearing the school uniform with the hem right down below my knees and carrying my lunch and books in a red suitcase that I thought was really cool, just like I had read about in books. The other kids didn't think it was cool though – they all had backpacks – and I knew I was in trouble. But Jan made sure she sat with me at lunch, and she shared her cupcake with me. She sat with me on the mat afterwards too, during story time, and we were fast friends from that day on. Different interests and different personalities but close friends none the less.

She knew what I needed the morning after the conference dinner. Turns out, one of the big things I needed was food. I had thrown out about half my lunch yesterday in order to save room for the delicious food at the conference dinner. The conference organisers had served us a roll, a muffin, a chocolate bar, and a piece of fruit in a brown paper bag for lunch – what was the message there? We're all back in school? – and as it turned out at the dinner I didn't eat anything other than that tiny quiche they served for starters. I'd had a bit to drink on an empty stomach too. So I wasn't feeling that great when I woke up. But coffee and bacon did their job and helped me to feel more with it.

The chat with Jan helped too.

'It was just so sudden, you know?'

'I'm sure it brought back a few memories'

'Yeah, it was so different but still, so much the same. I don't want to make this all about me, but it's really hard to get my head around it. I'm not coping with someone dying. Such a sudden death. So tragic.' I traced around the pattern on the table with my finger. Trying to focus, trying to pull myself together.

'So was it a heart attack?'

'I don't know. It looked like it. I hope they'll do an autopsy. He being a big shot international visitor and all. I'm wondering if there will be someone at the conference who would have more detailed information about why he died. I just feel like I need to know what happened. Is that bad?' I looked up at Jan.

'I'm sure that's not bad. It will help you to process, won't it?' her eyes were full of compassion.

'The thing is, I just don't understand how he could have had a heart attack. He was talking about how healthy he was, just before the dinner.'

He had been, too. Not talking to me, as such. It wasn't that I was good friends with Professor Conneally, far from it. It was just that we'd had a couple of hours to kill in between the conference and the dinner and Robbie, Misaki, and I had gone to find a pub close to the dinner venue where we could chill and drink, and a few others, including Conneally, had had the same idea. So we all stood around in a large group, drinks in hand or on the tall wooden tables, just chatting. Or in my case, just standing awkwardly.

I'm not my best in that situation, I mostly listen and try to feel like I am a part of the group. I wasn't really part of that group, I know, because when Conneally offered to buy the next round of drinks, I wasn't included in the offer. But then, neither were Robbie or Misaki. We were just postdoctoral hangers-on trying to get in on the professorial crowd.

One of the delegates – Ken Jones, a Tasmanian lecturer I remembered from my old biochemistry lectures – was included in the offer, but he passed on the beer in favour of an iced water. He was a short stocky guy in his fifties with hair like a wire brush. His request for water was met with a little gentle derision.

'No beer? Really?'

'No, not for me mate, thanks. I can't drink as much now, I had a triple bypass last year.'

'Whoah! How did that come about?' All the attention of anyone in earshot was now focussed on this story.

'I was in Singapore for three months and I was carrying some groceries back to my flat and suddenly I got a pain, right here' He drew a line across his chest, 'I stopped and put the bags down and it went away, I walked another 100 metres and the pain came back. I put the bags down and it went away again. Hmmm, I thought, I'll see a doctor about that when I get home. I stayed in Singapore about another month,' he was about to go straight on, like it was normal to completely ignore chest pain. Others didn't think it was quite so normal ...

'A month!' the mouthful of beer was nearly spat all over everyone in the close circle.

'Ha. Yeah, probably a bit longer than was good for me. Then I went home and the doctor did an angiogram, you know, up through the groin and stuff, and then he said, "I've got good news and bad news, the bad news is, I've only done one side so far and you have two blocked arteries, the good news: you're not dead!" Then they did the other side, and I didn't go home – straight into St Johns and had a triple bypass.'

'Wow. That's pretty full on.' No one was worried by the graphic details. I guess we were all scientists and pretty used to the gory or the detailed in one way or another.

'Yeah, so the doctor has told me to drink one glass of red a day.'

'Heh, or three or four ...' glasses were raised to his health and the conversation went on.

'How about you Conneally? Did you have a health scare? I hear you've taken up jogging.'

'Nah, nothing wrong with me – fit as a horse. I actually find that the jogging clears my mind, helps me do more work, you know? Time to myself to think without any inter-ruptions.'

'Oh really? That works? Maybe I'll have to take it up.'

'Yeah, it's not doing too badly for the old figure either – I can eat more at things like this. It's all a benefit.'

Professor Conneally laughed and patted his stomach and the discussion continued along the lines of diet and exercise. People love discussing what other people eat, I find. Even when you don't want it to be a point of discussion. But Professor Conneally seemed happy enough to share his fitness regime and diet. He was proud of it.

So I knew that he was looking after himself and I found it really strange that he would suffer a sudden heart attack when there was nothing wrong, when he was doing all the right things health-wise. Just so unexpected.

'Maybe he was exaggerating,' Jan said 'or sometimes people who were unhealthy and then take up jogging, they have heart attacks. They go for a jog, and fall down dead. It happens all the time.'

'You're right. I'm probably making too much of this. It's probably just one of those things that happen. Except ...'

'Except, what?'

'Except that he wasn't jogging. He was just eating his dinner!'

'What can I say? The thing is, he's gone. Worrying about how or why he died isn't going to bring him back. Sorry to be blunt, but ...'

'I know. I just wish I could find out what happened. I'm sure it would help me find closure. Do you think ... would Nate be able to find out anything?'

Nate is Jan's husband. He's a detective with the Hobart police force. Jan met him in Melbourne when she was at university and they moved back to Tassie after they got married. People do that a lot in Tassie – move away and then move back. The move back usually presages the birth of children, but I hadn't seen that with Jan and Nate yet. Not so much as a suspicion of a bump on Jan's gorgeously slim figure. They were young though. There was time.

'I guess so. There is bound to be an autopsy or a coroner's report or something. This guy is a big name, you tell me, and an overseas visitor. The thing is, I'm not sure if Nate will be able to tell you the outcome. It will probably be confidential. And you know Nate, he's a stickler for the rules.'

'Could you try him for me anyway? He might be able to just give you a nod or something and then you can tell me if it was all natural and stuff.'

'I'll try,' said Jan. She didn't look too happy about the request, but I have been receiving that look since primary school, and I knew she'd come through for me. But she had to check one more time, 'Are you sure this isn't just because he was giving you a job?'

'Oh, it might be.' I looked down at my hands, cupped around the coffee mug. She was right, I was probably paying too much attention to his death because it also changed my life; because Conneally's death had also destroyed the dreams I had of an exciting career in Cambridge.

One of Jan's staff called her to the register. She had a café to run and she'd spent too much time looking after me already. I sat and sipped my coffee and my thoughts went around and around, playing over every detail of the night before. The conversation with Misaki and Robbie, the scene at the VIP table – all the chatter and laughter cut short. The feeling of being outside in the cool evening air.

I thought about all the people who would be affected by the professor's death. I wondered whether Mrs Conneally had someone to look after her. Whether I could find her and offer my comfort and then just be there when she got the coroner's report ... But that was a bit mercenary, wasn't it? Latching on to someone and 'supporting' them for my own benefit, just so I could get answers.

Another sip of coffee and I realised that the conference was still going on. There was another day of talks booked, and I assumed they'd be holding them still. And Trudy would be there, and would be wondering what happened. She didn't make it to the dinner and she wouldn't know.

Robbie had asked her, 'Are you coming to the dinner tonight?' which was a bit of a mistake. Trudy works at the uni in Hobart, and is the primary carer for her four children, and always feels guilty for not giving more to one of those jobs or the other.

'Yeah, no, I can't come to the dinner, it all got too hard. I have to pick up one son from table tennis, then drop off another to band practice, then the grandparents are coming around for dinner and then I need to mark assignments.'

'Are you serious?! That's a crazy night!'

'That's pretty normal for Trudy' I'd said, 'she's superwoman.'

'Not really,' Trudy had looked humbly at the floor 'It could be just bad time management. There's always so much to do.'

'Nope, really superwoman,' I'd assured the rest of the bunch. 'Enjoy your night Trudy, we'll think of you as we eat and drink more than is good for us! We'll try not to feel too guilty!'

I felt guilty now. I should have rung her or something straight away, let her know what had happened. It's not fair that she's always the last to know just because she's so dedicated to her family. I shoved the last mouthful of bacon and egg into my mouth and swilled it down with the rest of the coffee. Then I headed to the conference centre.

The empty foyer of the conference venue had all the warmth and charm of a hospital waiting room, especially after the hospitality and comfort of The Lemon Tree. The large room was dotted with white plastic tables and around the edge the poster displays had big gaps, like missing teeth, where posters had been taken down prematurely. But maybe I was being unfair. At the beginning of the conference I had had no such reaction to the room.

That Wednesday morning when I had arrived, the first day of what I hoped would be a new start, I had been full of anticipation. After a year away from the academic scene, this was my first foray back in.

I remember the holiday atmosphere as the different conference delegates met and renewed connections from the last conference or caught up with lab and office mates after separation caused by differing travel schedules and hotel bookings. I had arranged to meet Trudy first thing but she was living up to her reputation of being late to everything and there had been no sign of her with twenty minutes to go before the first session. And to tell the truth, I enjoyed having some time alone to take it all in.

Snippets of conversation reached my ears: 'When did you arrive?'

'Two days ago – I've already done a bush walk, now I'm ready to sit for a while!'

'Tell me where you went! I'm heading out right after the conference.'

A far as I was concerned, that was a group doing exactly the right thing! Tasmania is awesome for nature lovers, but Hobart is a bit of a small town if you are into city life or night clubbing. Or whatever people do. I am the nature sort, myself. Or actually more the 'good book, comfortable chair and fireside' sort.

'How are you enjoying the weather, coming from Brisbane?'

'Is this summer? I'm wearing more layers than I usually wear in the winter.' The girl had wrapped her light jacket more tightly around herself.

'It's not so bad. It's pretty similar to the English summer, I'm feeling pretty much at home.'

I had decided to join this conversation, I didn't want my beloved state getting a bad name. I had just wandered up and joined in.

'It's not great weather right now but it should be better by the end of the week, you know, they say, if you don't like the Tassie weather, come back in five minutes.'

'Are you a local? How hot does it get here in summer?'

'Not real hot actually. We usually get about five very hot days and we always get a crash straight afterwards. We could have one day of 35 degrees but the next day will probably be 16.'

The girl from Brisbane shivered expressively but the English delegate was appreciative.

'That sounds pleasant – none of the tortuous long hot spells where you think you're going to pass out from the heat.'

'You get used to it. We all enjoy the heat but we only really like it for a day or so. The really fun bit is that the summer doesn't heat up properly until after the students go back to school in February. That's when we have our lovely hot days, and that's when the water has warmed up enough to go swimming. And there are all the students stuck in school. I remember being really put out about that as a kid.'

'You go swimming?' This was the girl from Brisbane. 'I dipped my toes in the water at the beach yesterday. It looks nice, yes, but it was freezing, so cold. I can't imagine anyone swimming here.'

'It's pretty cool, yep.' I nodded. 'Direct line to Antarctica. But you won't get a good picture of summer this week. December is reasonably volatile, weather-wise. We have even had snow for Christmas. In fact, in our newspaper we had a report of a UK family who came here for a holiday and experienced their first ever white Christmas.'

'Hopefully the weather will be decent on our afternoon off. It would be great if we could go up the mountain and actually see the view.'

'It doesn't sound like our chances are very good though. Knowing my luck it will be pouring with rain for the whole four hours I have to spend sight seeing.'

'I'll cross everything for you – fingers and toes. But you may just have to come down and visit again.'

The conversation felt like it was at an end and I was wondering how to bow out gracefully when I heard a yell in my general direction.

'Alicia! What are you doing here, Woman?'

'Robbie! Didn't you get my email?'

'What email? I haven't checked in the last week. I've been saving them for the boring sessions. No worries.' Robbie gave me a hug and checked in, 'how's life for you since you left the big city?'

'I tell you, I'm so enjoying the easier pace of life here. It's slower, but it's much more peaceful.'

I had decided that I would stay positive and keep my real thoughts about life to myself. I assumed that a few people would know that I left work because my Mum was sick. But they didn't need to know, really, about how I was feeling now. No-one would want to know about my grief, or my uncertainty about being able to go back to work, or my double-mindedness as to whether I even wanted to go back to work at a university. I would keep it light. At least until someone asked more deeply. And Robbie, friend though he was, was unlikely to ask more deeply.

'You'll be very glad to know that I've found a place to get good coffee, so the important things are taken care of. How has your year been?'

'Yeah, alright,' he said, 'I've had three papers published this year and there are another two in the pipeline so I'm a bit stuffed, to be honest. Five papers will do for one year don't ya think?'

Yes, I did think. This competition for more and more output was one thing about the academic career that I had found completely draining. Can't we just do the work creatively and see where it takes us? Keep it positive, keep it light I told myself, repeating it like a mantra. As far as encouraging me to get back into the scene, this was not a great start.

'What's the plan for next year?' I asked.

'Well, if there's funding then another couple of years as lab manager but I'm starting to look around for a more permanent place – I've had ten years already on short-term contracts.'

'I didn't realise you were on soft money there ...'

'Yeah, no security – two-year contracts at most. I'm starting to think industry might be the way to go. A good lab manager position in R&D in a pharma would be awesome, I just need time to start looking.'

I nodded, 'I get that. I hope you didn't come down here to look for work though. Tassie is not the place to be looking for an industry position – no big pharmaceutical companies here. But I hope you find someone here at the conference you can talk to, I'll keep an ear out for you. Robbie, you're being rude. Who's your friend?'

The young girl hanging around behind Robbie moved forward to say hello.

'Oh yeah, sorry. Lisa, this is my friend Alicia who has moved down to this backwater for a sea-change. Alicia, this is Lisa – I've just met her, she's a PhD student with Professor Conneally in Cambridge.'

'Hi Lisa, nice to meet you. Here's a fun fact: did you know that Conneally started his research life here in Tasmania?'

'No, really? That's amazing! Wow! I mean, here?! That's so awesome! I'll make sure I have a good look around now!'

'My friend Trudy (who should be turning up soon) works in the department where he used to work, she might be able to give you some insight into his character.'

Lisa laughed, 'I'm sure he was a party animal! Oh boy! A young Conneally, so much fun!'

'He's a party animal now,' agreed Robbie, 'especially during conferences – I remember being sucked into some late nights with the Conneally group, I even remember some Karaoke when we were in Osaka. I think he spent the whole conference wearing sun-glasses, he was so hungover. Good times, good times.'

'That sounds so great – Karaoke can be such fun!' Lisa let out an empty-headed giggle. I wondered what there was in her skull to enable the study of a PhD. It looked more like she was aiming for the role of Baywatch Girl more than serious scientist. Still, I wanted her to have a good time while she was here.

'I hope you can find something that's as much fun as that to do while you're in town. I can't speak about Karaoke bars as such, no idea if there even is one here. I always tell people that you come here for the bushwalking and the nature rather than the clubs and pubs. But maybe that's just me.'

'We saw a sign about whisky tasting, didn't we?' Robbie asked.

'Yes, on the way down here from the hotel. Don't worry, if there's fun, I'll find it.' Lisa said, and I could well believe it.

I had left them to it then, and gone to try to find Trudy. She had managed to get herself caught up in a crisis on the way from home to the conference and was running late, that was pretty normal for her. She made it though, just before the first session, and we had all gone in together, laughing and chatting, to hear the plenary lecture.

But now, this Friday morning, the conference venue had a completely different atmosphere. I wondered at first, as I looked around the empty foyer, if the rest of the conference had been cancelled. Then I heard a voice coming from the lecture theatre and realised that things were going on as planned. Duh, the foyer is always empty when all the conference delegates are in the lecture theatre listening to the talk.

Not that I wanted to join them, I sat instead on an uncomfortable plastic chair and mused about Conneally's strange death. Despite the coffee and the breakfast, I found myself dropping off to sleep. The lack of sleep the night before, coupled with the adrenalin draining away now that the emergency was over, meant that I was almost deep into dreamland when I was jolted back into the present by the sound of applause as the session ended.

The day after the conference dinner is usually poorly attended at any conference, and I always had sympathy for the presenter who got allocated the first presentation – the audience was either missing due to sleeping in, or hungover and not taking anything in at all. Today would have been even worse I guessed, and the numbers coming out of the lecture theatre showed me to be correct. There were only about a third of the attendees that had been present the day before.

Trudy was there though, and I pulled myself out of my chair to go and say hello.

'Small crowd today.'

'Yes. I didn't hear about Professor Conneally until I turned up this morning. They gave an announcement just before the first session.'

I really felt guilty then. I should have rung her last night. What kind of friend am I leaving her out of the loop when something this big had happened?

'Oh Trudy, I'm so sorry, I didn't even think to ring you.'

'That's fine Alicia, truly. It must have been awful being there. You would have been busy just coping yourself.' Trudy gave me a hug and we wandered back to a table.

'It wasn't great. Have many speakers cancelled today?'

'Not too many gaps, no. And we're all staying to hear the people who want to speak anyway. Why should they miss out on sharing their work? Especially if they didn't know Professor Conneally personally. It's tragic, but it's just one of those things. They're going to name a prize after him.' We sat in the uncomfortable plastic seats, as far away from the general crowd as possible.

'Yeah, I thought they might do something like that. Well, it's definitely a conference dinner that will go down in history. I'm not sure that it's limited to being just a tragic death, either' I mused, half to myself.

Trudy sat up, 'Alicia, what are you saying?'

'Oh, nothing. Nothing. Don't worry about it. Forget I said anything.' I hadn't really intended to say it out loud, and I was surprised to hear the words coming out of my mouth. But something was coalescing in my brain, an idea that wouldn't go away.

'Tell me everything, how did it happen?'

Quietly, in murmurs, I described the scene at the restaurant the night before. And as I repeated the story, and thought about how healthy Conneally was, my suspicions crystallised. Surely there was more to this death than just a tragic health issue. There was something wrong. Just what I was supposed to do with my hunch, though, I didn't have a clue. And as the coffee wore off, I found it harder and harder to think at all.

The bell rang for the start of the next session and Trudy asked if I was coming back in as I failed to stifle a yawn.

'No, I won't. I think you're doing the right thing, but I can't face this right now. In fact, I think the thing I need to do is go home and get a bit more sleep. I'll catch up with you soon.'

I gave her a hug and wandered back to my car, my home, and my bed.

I lay in bed, trying to nap, but I couldn't sleep. It was totally unfair. I felt so tired, but as soon as I laid my head on my pillow a thousand thoughts came rushing at me. The picture of Conneally grabbing his chest and falling backwards, his weeping wife, the reactions around the rest of the table.

It came to me that there were some strange reactions when you thought about who was sitting at that main table. For example, there was Brasindon, the other big-name professor. He had known Conneally since their under-grad days. You would have thought he'd have shown some concern, but when things happened, he looked on with an almost blank face, he was not upset at all.

But then, the two professors weren't the best of friends. Misaki had told me that there was history between them that went way back.

You see, Misaki had completed her undergraduate degree at the University of Sydney, as had Brasindon and Conneally years before. And Misaki (being the super student that she is) had won a university medal. She had looked up who the previous winners were and had found out that both Professor Brasindon and Professor Conneally had won a medal in the same year. She told me that the talk around the university was that they had been in competition ever since.

And now I came to think of it, Conneally's talk also showed that friction.

His lecture had been the first talk of the conference, a position of eminence. And he was an excellent choice for first speaker. He had woven applications to every day life into the text, given heaps of acknowledgement to his students and postdoc staff, and peppered the talk with interesting anecdotes about various big names at the conference. He began his talk with a photo of his group in Hobart ten years ago. He pointed out key people that were still working at the uni – not many names I recognised but that made sense – he was biochemistry after all, I was chemistry. Trudy was nodding though – Ken Jones, Joshua Hume, she was laughing at how much they'd changed.

The next photo was an even older photo of Brasindon and Conneally from their undergraduate days. From where I was sitting I could see Professor Brasindon grimace when the photo came on the screen – it was obvious that while Conneally had aged gracefully, Brasindon had not. Conneally still had all his hair, and was looking pretty slim and stylish. Brasindon, on the other hand, had changed to become dumpy and bald (with that really un-stylish ring of longish grey hair around the back of his head) and, well, you know, beige. And he did not appreciate the joke at his expense.

Professor Brasindon's lecture after morning tea that day had been a complete change from the Conneally lecture. I had lost interest in the first five minutes, ate about fifteen mints with the accompanying competition with myself as to how quietly I could open each wrapper, thought through my life plans and wondered whether I really wanted to get back into academia if it meant sitting through any more talks like this, ran over the list of academics at the conference I wanted to talk to, tried to stop multiple yawns (unsuccessfully), and basically lost forty five minutes of my life. I decided that every conference talk I sat through in the future would be measured for boredom on a scale from Brasindon to Conneally.

I spent a fair bit of the talk people-watching. Most of the rows were crammed full and most of us were making ourselves as small as possible so as not to impinge on the personal space of our neighbours. People were curling up in a ball so they could make notes without jutting out an elbow, or stacking bags in front of their feet and destroying their already tiny foot space. But just in front of me was someone taking up three chairs. It's not that he was in any way overweight – it wasn't the obese type of spread – he was just very relaxed. His arms reached out over the backs of the neighbouring chairs on each side and his legs spread wide, even his hair was taking up more space than it should – some women would kill for full bodied hair like that. I wondered if he came in early to reserve the chairs for himself, and whether his ego was as large as his hair.

A few seats over from the guy with the abundant hair was a stressed-out post doc, trying to write a paper on his laptop unobtrusively while pretending to listen to the talk. He was glancing up at the professor or the big screen every now and then but his fingers were going all the while and his concentration was elsewhere. I didn't blame him. When a deadline was looming, a week spent listening to others' research was a bit much. There was no harm done there.

Looking to the left past a few dedicated note takers, there was a professor checking his email. He was obviously not listening at all. Sitting in the lecture theatre was the level of courtesy he was willing to offer, listening would be too much to ask. He was a busy man who was at the conference to network and talk about his own research, not to listen to anything out of field. I wondered whether Prof

Brasindon would do the same thing himself. He seemed like that kind of guy – full of his own importance.

I turned my attention back to the front. Was there anything interesting being said? No, not that I could tell, and also, I'd lost the thread now, I didn't have the background information to make sense of any of the talk anymore.

'So as you can see here, the longer side-chain makes the difference and with the new set you can see the overlap here. Compared to the information on the previous table ...' my attention drifted again.

Just then I noticed someone creeping in through the side entrance, down the front of the auditorium near the stage. It was pretty late to be coming in, the session was nearly over. I looked at him unthinkingly for a while. If people came in during a talk they did tend to stand there rather than interrupting the talk by finding a seat, but then, they also tended to look at the speaker. This guy was scanning the audience, like he was looking for someone.

Behind his shoulder, someone else turned up. A little blonde slip of a girl. He was pointing someone out to her – I couldn't tell who it was from that angle. Did he have a friend at the conference? My curiosity well and truly piqued I made a mental note to look them up in the meal break and ask.

I was just telling myself, 'only question time to go, just a few more minutes of questions and then you can get out of here, just hold on – coffee is only moments away' when Trudy raised her hand to ask a question. I'm not kidding. She had actually listened to the talk and digested it enough to ask something about it. I roused myself and tried to force my slack-jawed sleepy countenance into something looking intelligent and aware – Trudy was sitting right next to me and the attention of the whole room was now focussed my way. Not a good time to let what I was feeling show on my face.

'This may be a stupid question, but what was the control used for the experiments on slide seven?'

That was impressive – Trudy had managed to make her way past the formidable boredom of a bad speaker to find the fruit of the talk, or so it appeared to me. Professor Brasindon was not of the same opinion.

'That's a first year undergraduate concept, I will not bother to answer, you can ask someone at your institution later.'

Trudy's face turned beetroot-red. I didn't need to feign alertness anymore. You could hear the collective gasp echo across the room. No one could believe that he had been so rude. Even if they agreed with what he said, there was no need to say it like that. The general rule, followed in polite society, was that you answered politely and then talked to your friends about how bad you thought the question was afterwards. You never said anything so insulting out loud. Even the chair of the session was taken aback.

'Um, ok,' he stuttered, 'are there any other questions?'

Needless to say, there were no more questions. Who would dare?

I was anxious for Trudy, 'Are you ok?' I asked as we waited with the crowd to leave the room.

'Yes, yes, I'm fine, I didn't mean to be so stupid.'

We edged our way out of the row of seats and progressed slowly, pushed along with the rest of the crowd down the steps to the exit.

'You were not stupid!' I exclaimed. 'He didn't explain himself well enough, he was a dreadful speaker. Anyway, anyone has the right to ask a question and be answered – he had no right to treat you so badly.' And on and on I raved as we nudged our way out, proclaiming loudly what a horrible little man he was.

Eventually (far too late) I noticed the horror dawning on Trudy's face. I turned, and there, right behind me, was Professor Brasindon. His eyes met mine, he must have heard what I said, but he didn't comment. I turned back to Trudy, grabbed her hand and forced our way through the crowd into the foyer, my face was now the one burning with embarrassment.

Once we were safely away Trudy laughed at me.

'Alicia! You pick your times.'

'Well, he needed to hear it.' I stated, much braver now that he wasn't anywhere around.

'I stand by what I said, he was rude. Come on Trudy, we're going for coffee, I've had enough of this for now, we can come back for the afternoon session, but right now it's a good time for a break.'

We grabbed Robbie and Misaki as we passed through the foyer and headed to The Lemon Tree for a decent coffee and debrief.

They all agreed with me on the way to the café. Brasindon (we didn't think he was worthy of the appellation of 'professor' any more) was the rudest man we had met. And the worst speaker. We had no idea what he was trying to say in his talk. Misaki even proposed that he didn't understand the work himself and was trying to hide his incompetence. And we all agreed that he must have felt like he was being shoved into Conneally's shadow.

As I lay in my bed the day after the dinner, the afternoon sunshine pouring through the window, the whole situation became clear. Brasindon worked in a Biochemistry Department in a university – he could have made some poison that would have killed Conneally. Brasindon hated the man – that much was clear. And Brasindon was sitting at the same table – he could have easily dropped something into Conneally's plate.

Maybe that's why I felt like something was so wrong. Maybe it was just possible that Conneally was poisoned. That his death wasn't a natural thing that happened because of a blood clot or whatever. Maybe Brasindon, spurred on by the laughter in the lecture, decided now was the time, and that Conneally had to die.

I needed to talk to Nate.

'It has to be Brasindon.'

'Who? What? The love of your life?' Jan had answered the door to my fierce banging and answered my statement with a cheeky smile, but I was not going to be dissuaded.

'No, the murderer.'

'Alicia, come in, sit down, and tell me what you're on about. Would you like a drink? Can I get you anything to eat?'

I did as I was told. And once I was safely ensconced in Jan's comfortable red leather recliner and she had brought us both some sparkling water, she asked again what was going on.

'So is this the death of Professor Conneally that you're thinking about?'

'Brasindon did it, I'm sure.'

'That, Honey, is a major conclusion jump. Let's start at the beginning. Why do you think it's murder, again?'

'Right, well, everyone thinks it's a heart attack, right? What do you need to have a heart attack?'

'I guess most of the time you've eaten fatty foods, not exercised, and you get blocked arteries.'

'Exactly. But he had talked about how much he had exercised and how healthy he was.'

'He could have been boasting. Lots of people make stuff up like that.'

'Ye... es,' I considered that for about two seconds, 'but Trudy said that he looked much more healthy than he had before. No I think he was really healthy. So why did his heart stop? And why so suddenly? He must have been poisoned.'

'Hun that's still a bit of a jump.'

'Why else would he die so suddenly? I wish I could get my hands on some evidence – do some scientific tests or see a scan or something. But I'm sure he was poisoned. The more I think about it the more sure I am.'

Jan was silent, so I took her silence for consent and continued to think out loud.

'So which poison do we think? If it were cyanide, his lips would be blue, arsenic would have given him stomach cramps, vomiting and other symptoms you don't want me to mention. Potassium chloride would have stopped the heart, but it would have to be given intravenously – a little difficult in the restaurant situation. Maybe a pesticide? Some sort of nerve agent? It's not something common, that's for sure.'

'Ok, settle down just a little. Now stop me if I've got this wrong but if I've heard you correctly, what we have so far is that he HAS to have been poisoned, but you have no idea what poison would have been used, or why, or how, or who.'

'Uh, no, back up there a bit. I reckon I know why. Brasindon! That's who and that's why. He has got sick of the rivalry and decided to take out his major rival once and for all.'

'Alicia, if you really think this is true, maybe you should go to Nate and tell him. But are you sure this is not just a, well, you don't like Brasindon very much, do you?'

No I didn't like Brasindon, and Jan knew it. She'd been there for the conversation in the café after Brasindon's talk. And Trudy hadn't been able to wait to tell her my faux pas. She was calling out to Jan before the tinkle of the café doorbell had finished sounding.

'Jan, you won't believe what Alicia just did.'

My face had burned again with embarrassment and I busied myself organising a table for us all as Trudy explained to everyone how Brasindon found out just what I thought of his rudeness.

'Oh wow, Alicia. How to win friends and influence people.'

'That's just stunning. Well done.' The laughter at my misfortune let me know that this moment would be relived in every conference in my future. But having said that, everyone agreed with me, and the four of us went on to pull Brasindon's character apart completely.

'We know for sure now he's been told off for that particular bit of poor behaviour. Pity no-one's told him off for his other faults.'

'What, like his unutterably boring lecturing style? Or his incredibly poor fashion sense?'

'I hear Brasindon was pissed that Conneally's lecture was scheduled first.' Robbie said, 'It makes sense to me though – I don't think Brasindon should have been given the forty five minutes, twenty would have been more than enough.'

Brasindon and Conneally were unquestionably contrasting people – Brasindon was a harsh, all business, very head down, introverted, only-talk-to-me-about-work kind of guy. We wondered about his home life-what his wife was like and how she coped with him. And we compared him (exceedingly unfavourably) with Professor Conneally – friendly, fun, supportive to his students.

'But Trudy, how about the leopard?' asked Misaki.

'What leopard?' asked Jan.

'Oh, yeah, we were talking about Conneally before the lecture, how he used to use people on his climb up the career ladder. Before, back when he was working here in Tassie. Trudy was saying that a leopard can't change his spots.'

'It's true, I thought that. But compared with Brasindon, I mean, at least he has some social skills. Brasindon stomps on everyone's heads whether they get him to the top or not.'

'Conneally has social skills alright,' said Robbie, 'he thinks he's a young gun still. Trying to party with the students. I mean, he's old now. He should just stay old. Hang with the old folk, not try to cut it with the crowd.'

'Maybe that's why he's been looking after himself a bit more – so that he can still run with the young crowd,' said Trudy. That caught everyone's attention. We plied her with questions and she told us that she hardly recognised Conneally when he first got up to talk – he looked so different from how she remembered him from a conference five years ago – much fitter, slimmer and healthier. We all agreed again, now that she mentioned it, he did look like someone who was taking the time to look after himself. It was good to see someone going well in their career without giving up on every other part of life to focus on work.

'That's what it comes back to, Jan. Conneally was looking after himself. He shouldn't have died.'

'Maybe not, but these things happen, and you can't blame Brasindon just because you think he's a horrible little man.'

I was taken aback. Jan wasn't agreeing with me. She always agreed with me. For heaven's sake, when I tried to convince the class in Grade 3 that Santa was real she agreed with me. What was going on? Maybe I was being too enthusiastic, maybe I was sounding hysterical.

In a much more measured voice I said, 'I can see what you're thinking. And yes, I don't like the guy. But I heard that he and Conneally had been in competition all their professional lives. I am still sure that Brasindon is the one responsible. He is the only one who hated Professor Conneally. Everyone else loved him. Who else would have a motive?'

Jan sighed, 'Well, I guess the best thing we can do is take your suspicions to Nate. He would know what to do with them.'

'That's true. I'll do that. Do you think he'll mind talking tonight? It's a bit after office hours.'

'There are no office hours when something like this is on the table, don't worry. He should be back here soon; you can have a chat to him when he turns up. I can't promise anything, but at least you'll have given the information to the right person. Why don't you come into the kitchen with me? We can chat while I make dinner.'

It was a little awkward between us then, just waiting for Nate to show up. But I perched myself on a kitchen stool while Jan peeled and sliced vegetables and braised the meat for an aromatic stew. I was in awe, as usual, when I watched her in the kitchen. She used herbs and spices I never knew existed. I watched her and wondered whether there were spice bottles hidden away in my kitchen somewhere that Mum had bought in the far distant past and never used. I certainly had never used them. You didn't need them to make sausage and mash, or frozen meals – for – one.

We were quiet for a while, then Jan started a new topic that I could really get into.

'How did Trudy's talk go?'

Trudy had given a twenty-minute presentation at the conference on the Thursday afternoon before the conference dinner. Well, it was supposed to be twenty minutes.

'Oh man. Jan, it was awful. She just went on and on, I didn't know how to look her in the face afterwards.'

'Oh no.' Jan was more concerned about this than about Conneally's death. But then, she had never met Conneally.

'She started well, really explained the theory behind the research so clearly that anyone could understand it, but then, oh dear, she took too long over that and too long to explain everything. She just went on and on. The chair tried to wind her up and she said, 'just a bit more' and kept going. Then he stood beside her to make her stop and still she kept going, by the end she was gabbling away really fast but she just kept going, making sure she finished Every. Single. Slide.'

'What did you say to her?'

'Nothing. I just gave her a wan "well done". I didn't know what to say. I mean her research was good, but not good enough to cut into the afternoon break for.'

'I guess it's just Trudy's bad sense of time.'

'I guess so. I think the way to go about it is to complain about someone else who does the same thing. Maybe she'll get the message obliquely. I don't want to hurt her.'

'Possibly ...'

'Anyway, I was lucky really. The talk after hers was worse so I could complain about that instead.'

'How could it be worse?'

'It was an honours student. The research was bad. The presentation was dreadful. She didn't go overtime, but she read the whole thing word for word from a piece of paper she was holding. The paper was shaking so much that she had trouble reading it and her laser pointer was shaking so much we could barely work out which bit of the slide she was pointing at. Poor thing, she was so nervous.'

'Glad I didn't have to sit through that.'

'It made sense of something for me though ... she was the girl I had seen in Brasindon's lecture, watching a movie with her headphones in both ears.'

'Watching a movie? During a talk?'

'Yep! I couldn't believe it myself, but then if she was an honours student it makes a bit more sense.'

'Maybe, but it's rude nevertheless.'

'Absolutely. I was wishing you were there so that I had someone to roll eyes with.'

'Naww, that's sweet – cynicism buddies, that's what we are.'

A car pulled into the driveway.

'That's Nate – hang here, I'll just let him know what's going on.'

Jan walked to the door and let Nate in. I could hear a quick murmur of conversation from Jan and Nate's 'Really? Now?' in response. He didn't sound that impressed.

But I was there for a reason. And that reason came out the instant he walked into the room.

'Hi Nate, I want to report a murder.'

'How about I dish us up some dinner and Alicia, you can tell Nate what you're thinking,' said Jan and disappeared into the kitchen. She left the door open though, I think she wanted to hear what was going on.

I explained my theory again; the health of Professor Conneally, the sudden death, the possibility of poison.

'And the only person I have seen in the whole conference who has anything against Prof Conneally is Brasindon, Professor Brasindon. The two have been rivals for years, since their undergrad degrees. And Brasindon is such a horrible person, I can imagine him doing anything. He's so cold blooded.'

'Look, are you sure you're not just taking offence? I know he's treated Trudy badly (Jan told me about that) but a cutting comment is a little different to killing someone in real life.'

'Nate, they have history. History! Going right back to their undergrad.'

Nate smiled, 'that's a lot of history.' Then he became more serious. 'I'm sure you've seen on TV how a case can be thrown out because all the evidence is circumstantial? Well, I hate to break it to you Alicia, but you don't even have circumstantial evidence. I can't go around arresting people because someone has a hunch. There has to be at least some evidence. You don't even know that this was a murder.'

'But – he said he was healthy.'

'Look, Professor Conneally, he's a big name foreign visitor. He's died suddenly, there will definitely be a post-mortem and a report for the coroner. In fact, I've been asked to help out with the report. People will be looking into it. The coroner will find out if there's evidence of foul play. How about you just let us do our job?'

'Yes, Jan and I had talked about that. Do you think that when the results come through you could let me know whether the death was natural or not? I'm sure it's not but it would be great to get confirmation.'

'Alicia, look, I'm sorry, but these things are confidential. I can't go sharing them with every man and his dog. I'm sure you under-stand that it just isn't possible. Just trust us.

We know what we're doing. Are you sure you're not taking things to heart because of your Mum?'

I'd like to say that I responded maturely, I could see his point, I agreed with him and backed down. And I'd like to say that I then stayed with them and had a lovely meal and chat and that I went to bed and slept soundly that night. But it turns out that I'm not as mature as I would like to be.

Instead, I just felt embarrassed, that I'd been fobbed off, treated like a preschooler. I was angry and upset. I felt sure that both Jan and Nate thought I was insane.

Feeling my face grow hot, and swallowing tears that threatened to break through, I said thanks but no thanks to Jan's invitation to dinner and left them to it.

I was so disappointed that they weren't on my side, that they weren't willing to work with me to find the evidence. I knew that the incident with Trudy's question in the lecture wasn't that big a deal, but I thought it was an outworking of Brasindon's character. If you have no respect for anyone then it's a short step to getting those you don't like out of your way, isn't it?

I walked down to the beach, hoping the evening breeze would cool my face and that the walk would help me pull myself together. I must have looked a strange sight, pounding my way up and down the beach until I had walked off all the frustration. But as my feelings cooled I slowed down a bit and tried to think it all through again.

Nate and Jan were right, of course, there was no evidence, I had jumped to conclusions, and it was probably due to losing Mum and to losing face in front of Brasindon. An accusation of murder is a huge thing and you can't just do it because things feel wrong. I had been too strong in saying what I said to them. For some reason I had decided that talking like I was absolutely sure was the way to convince them that something was worth investigating. But instead, I had come across as unhinged and insane. And probably more insane because of the way I left so abruptly. What an idiot I was. There was no way that Nate would follow up on anything now. He was a sensible man and would sensibly put everything I had said out of his mind.

I wished I could put things out of my mind.

Why couldn't I just let it go, just say that he died and it was a tragedy and that was the end of it?

But I couldn't. The death felt wrong. I had a hunch that there was something dodgy about Professor Conneally's death and I couldn't get rid of that feeling no matter how scientific I tried to be. This went against all my training but it wouldn't go away. I had to find evidence. But how?

Jan closed the front door and leaning against it, looked back at Nate.

'She was pretty upset,' she said.

'Hmmm,' answered Nate.

'Could there be anything in it? I mean, could there?'

'No. Of course not. He's just had a heart attack or something. It happens.'

Both of them trailed back down the hallway and sat at the dining table. They looked at their meals but neither of them felt much like eating.

'She is very upset though,' said Nate.

'She really is.'

'I tell you what, I'll look into it thoroughly. If I can find out exactly what happened then we might be able to calm her down, stop her thinking about it. At the very least I can make sure there's absolutely no sign of foul play.'

'That would be so good. I'm a bit worried she'll stop talking to us over this one, and I'd hate for that to happen.'

'Yeah, me too. I'll give it a good go. I'll make sure I get the coroner's report first thing and go over it with a fine-toothed comb. We'll be able to sort it out, I'm sure.'

He took a mouthful of the stew.

'Man. How do you do this? Turning food into nectar of the gods? This is good. Are you going to eat?'

'Yeah, I think I can now. Thanks Nate. And let me know how you get on too will you? I'm curious now too.'

'No problem. As much as I can. Without giving away confidential information. You know how it is.'

'Yes, Nate. I know how it is.' Jan gave him a loving slap and got on with her food.

The next morning it was hard for me to get going. The conference was over. I had nowhere to go and nothing to do. I had a hunch I wanted to work on but I just wasn't sure what to do with it.

One thing I was sure of, I didn't want to go back to The Lemon Tree. I would need to find a new place to have a morning coffee. It was just too embarrassing to go and see Jan. She'd ask if I was ok, if I'd changed my mind, and I'd have to try to explain that while I could see her point, I was sticking to my guns. For no reason I could understand. And I didn't really want to face up to the kind of person I'd been the night before. I decided to start looking for a new café straight away.

Kingston Beach is a tiny little township on the bank of the Derwent River. The speed limit is 40 km/h for the whole suburb. There is no industry, just cottage crafts and eateries. It isn't really a place, just an extension of a place. For groceries, or petrol, or anything really, you head into Kingston itself. For business you follow the Derwent into Hobart, Tasmania's tiny capital.

One thing I loved about The Lemon Tree was that it was just around the corner from my little cottage. I could walk along the river bank, enjoy the sight of children playing in the playground or kayakers on the river, I could even feed the ducks if I wanted to be mobbed by angry squawking birds. And then right there was decent coffee and delicious food. But it wasn't that much further to find another café. I would just have to get in the car.

I headed away from Kingston Beach and into Hobart proper. There had to be heaps of places that would be pleasant to sit in, drink a coffee, write in a journal for a while. And Hobart wasn't that far from home – it only took ten minutes to drive in, especially if you waited for the peak-hour traffic to pass. Or maybe I should call it peak-minute traffic – there really aren't that many people in this tiny state I call home.

I headed to the Hobart waterfront and after a short wander, decided I could take a chance on a café called (fittingly) Waterfront. It couldn't have been more different to The Lemon Tree. From the tinkle of the bell as you open the door to the dining room in The Lemon Tree you feel at home. The furniture is mismatched chairs and tables from the 60s, the walls are a warm red, the L-shaped room is always full of a variety of people. There are often mothers' groups seated around the big table, the strollers lined up against the wall and the older children running in and out of the play room on the side. The seats outside are taken by dog walkers and the dogs wish you good morning as you walk in. There are smaller tables where older couples sit and enjoy the sunshine and a good coffee. There are couples eagerly conversing over shared slices of cake. It's a friendly environment, a homey place.

The café I found myself in this Saturday morning was not of the same ilk. The tables were square and black, the chairs were black leather, the customers didn't look relaxed at all. Even if they were sharing a table, there was no conversation. They were just staring at their phones or reading a paper. The music was loud. The servers didn't smile. And the coffee, ugh, the milk was overheated, the beans themselves must have been super-poor quality, it tasted dreadful.

I felt I was paying a penance of some sort. I wanted to run back to The Lemon Tree and tell Jan, 'I'm sorry, you're right, there's nothing to look into at all. I'll just stop worrying about it.' But that would be giving up on my integrity. I believed that Conneally's death was strange, that maybe it was even murder, and I couldn't just shove something like that under the mat. I wanted Jan and Nate to take me seriously, I wanted to be right about this.

Which was bad, wasn't it? The thing was, it would be better (in the big picture) if I was wrong about the whole situation, and that no-one had committed a murder. But I was sure I was right. I just needed to find some evidence.

There was a newspaper on my table and I picked it up and flicked through it looking for anything that might be about Conneally's death. On page four I saw the tiniest little paragraph:

Death a Shock for Conference Goers

Professor James Conneally, (61) from England passed away suddenly while attending a dinner at the International Biosciences Conference in Hobart on Thursday night. His death is believed to be of natural causes. 'He will be sorely missed,' stated Dr Ken Jones of The University of Tasmania 'it will be a great loss to the biochemistry community.' Professor Conneally was once an employee of The University of Tasmania but has since moved to Cambridge University where he investigated the causes and treatment of Motor Neurone Disease. A report is being prepared for the Coroner.

Well, that was no help. It didn't give me any information I didn't already know. The journalist had not even been nosey enough to find out about the tension between Conneally and Brasindon. Was I the only one thinking it was strange how he died?

Well, yes. Yes I was.

What was wrong with me?

The café had been filling up as I had been musing to myself and I looked up from the newspaper to find an impeccably dressed English woman asking to share my table. And being me, I couldn't say no.

'Yes, of course,' I said, like it was all I had ever wanted. Like sharing my quiet coffee table with a complete stranger was the first thing on my bucket list. But then I realised it was a good thing, because the tall, slim, ramrod straight lady in the peach and grey twin suit with the string of pearls, her greying hair tied up in a tight bun, and a red slash of lipstick defining her downturned mouth, was Mrs Brasindon. I knew her from the conference dinner – she had been sitting on the VIP table next to her husband. Sitting still and upright and not talking to anyone around her. She had fallen into my lap (so to speak; it might have made conversation a little more difficult if that were literally the case) and I took her presence to be a sign from the heavens and started investigating.

I pointed out the newspaper article and introduced myself and made noises about how I was a delegate at the conference, and wasn't it a dreadful thing to have happened.

'I suppose it was,' she responded, 'but I can't say I'm sorry that Conneally is dead.'

'Oh ... um ... you didn't like him much then?' I was a bit taken aback by how cold she was.

'Do I look like the kind of person who would 'like' someone like him? I don't think so.'

'I didn't realise he was so awful, I'm sorry, I didn't know him very well.' I mean, I was willing to go and work for him, but one conversation about work options in the future doesn't count as a meaningful relationship, does it?

Mrs Brasindon's order arrived – loose-leaf tea in a red china pot, and a jug of milk on the side. Maybe this place should have been called a tea-shop and not a coffee-shop – they obviously took more care with their tea.

'Well,' said Mrs Brasindon, slightly mollified by the appearance of a proper teapot, 'he didn't show his real character to most people. People are very happy to look at the jolly exterior and ignore his avarice and poor work practices.'

'I thought that, forgive me, but I thought that Professor Brasindon and Professor Conneally were long time friends ...'

'They've been colleagues for a long time, but I would not say that they were friends. When I see how that Conneally hurt my husband, well, how could we be friends? I ask you.' Then she tutted – she actually tutted. Properly English.

'He was treated badly then?'

'I probably shouldn't say anything, but I can't let everyone think he was an angel. You would think so, the way people are talking.'

'They always do that after someone dies, don't they? The person immediately gets put on a pedestal – the good is magnified and the bad is forgotten.'

'I don't have enough good to remember for that to happen. No, I prefer to think of people, alive or dead, for who they really are.'

It took a bit of wangling and working but I finally got the story out of Mrs Brasindon. It would have been so much easier if I were a detective. I had to pretend that I cared, and for someone like this ice-block of a woman that wasn't easy to do. But in the end she told me what she was so upset about.

'Conneally decided that he and my husband should do a joint funding application. That they had worked in the same area for so long that they would have a better chance of getting the funding – some centre of excellence or institute for something – or – other – if they worked together.'

'Did it work? Was it successful?'

'What didn't work was the 'work together' part. My husband did all the application work. He slaved for the funding, worked his fingers to the bone. Conneally did nothing. Nothing that I could see. But does that get taken into account when funding is approved? Not one bit. If the money was distributed according to who had done the most work, then my husband would be receiving all of it, but no, there was Conneally demanding half of the money, demanding "his share". It makes me furious.'

And there was the motive. More motive even than I had seen before. Money. It's always about money. If Professor Brasindon was half as angry as his wife then I could see anything happening.

'How does Professor Brasindon feel about all that? It sounds very unfair, I bet he was upset when he heard how it was all going to pan out.' That's me, putting on my best TV detective impression.

'Oh no, not my husband. He is so generous, so kind natured.'

'Oh, that's ... good.'

I didn't know what to say, this picture of Brasindon was so different to the picture I had in my head. I tried to keep an open mind but to accept this picture, well, my mind might have to be so open that my brains fell out!

'Yes, my husband only cares about the research. He is completely dedicated. In fact, he was very happy to have the funding approved and he told me that he didn't mind where the research would be conducted, as long as it was being performed so that science would benefit.'

'Wow. He sounds like a very good man.'

Too good to be true, really. It was a bit like Lizzie Bennett meeting Mr Darcy's house-keeper at Pemberley. Which picture of Professor Brasindon was correct? The jealous, enraged murderer, or the dedicated generous researcher?

'He's a caring, considerate man. He looks after me, looks after his students.'

'He has good relationships with his students then?'

'Yes, but just as a teacher – a good supervisor, nothing like that Conneally. His poor wife is probably much better off now.'

I nodded encouragingly, like I had been for the whole conversation, and then the words filtered into my brain and I shook my head to clear it.

'I'm sorry, what do you mean? Isn't she worse off?'

'Well, I don't mean to be a gossip ...'

No, of course not.

'But the man treated her dreadfully. Have you seen how he flirts with all his students? I'm sure there was something going on between him and that girl Lisa – she's always wearing those high skirts and low tops – just trying to get her degree by, well do I need to say? I'm sure you know how these tarty girls get their way. She's just the type. And he's the type to let it all happen. His poor wife, having to put up with that. If I were in her place, well, let's just say I'd be happier now that he's dead.'

I didn't really know what to say to that. I decided that Professor and Mrs Brasindon were well suited they were both as unpleasant as each other. I didn't like either of them. I was ready to exit this conversation, investigation or no investigation.

And then things got worse.

'Why are you talking to her?'

I looked up and there was Professor Brasindon himself looking at me like I was a slug that his wife had pulled out of the garden. Obviously he recognised me. I really should have been more careful about opening my big mouth after his presentation. I should have at least made sure he wasn't anywhere around.

'Darling, this is Dr Alicia Conway ...'

'I don't care what her name is, I don't understand why you are talking to her.'

'Well, I was just explaining to her how that horrible Conneally has mistreated you with the funding application. And that we're better off now that he's gone.'

'You know nothing. We were perfectly placed to work together on the project. Now he is gone the funding has fallen through and I will have to start the messy business of funding applications all over again. But why I'm explaining this to her,' he nodded in my general direction, 'I don't know. It's none of anyone's business. We're leaving. Now.'

Mrs Brasindon took a last sip of her tea and calmly gathered her things. Then without so much as a glance at me she followed her husband out of the café.

And I sat, feeling like I had been hit by a brick.

I could see that I might have been a bit hasty in accusing Brasindon of murder and I was, to be honest, a little more worried about what Nate and Jan would be thinking of me. If Conneally had been murdered now I could see that there might be a second very reasonable motive. If I thought back through the week, taking Mrs Brasindon's gossip into account, I could see that Conneally had taken special notice of Lisa – mentioning her several times in his talk, to the point where Trudy, Misaki and I had found it noteworthy and discussed it in the break after Conneally's lecture.

'I'm just wondering who the student "Lisa" is that he kept talking about?' asked Trudy.

'She's that girl just over there – the one in the heels. Robbie introduced us before you turned up.'

'Well, he thinks she's the best thing since sliced bread. She's definitely his pet student.'

'I hear that they are closer than they should be just for work,' said Misaki, 'when there's a group party or drinks after work those two are always there and they are always the last two left ...'

'Surely that's just gossip though, maybe the group is just jealous of her success,' I said.

'Where there's smoke there's fire,' said Trudy, 'I mean, look at the length of her skirt! Or is it a belt? And her earrings.'

'Hmmm, maybe. We don't all have to give up on fashion, just because we're academics.'

'What are you trying to say, Alicia? Are you saying we're all dowdy here?'

I looked at my friends – Trudy was wearing white capri pants, and an aqua long top over a white singlet. Her strawberry-blonde hair fell in loose curls down her back. Misaki's cat shaped earrings fell just below her glossy black hair. She wore a pink shirt with white polkadots and black shorts and sandals. They both out-did me – I was in my normal jeans and t-shirt, my uniform for almost every situation, my mousey brown hair pulled back into a ponytail. I always felt tall and bland and awkward around them. Not that I was a giant or anything, but I wasn't the petite and skinny class of person and there was no point in dressing like I was.

'Well, obviously, I wasn't talking about you at all – maybe about me. But you know the stereotypical female scientist that's totally given up on worrying about her looks. Wears an ill-fitting plaid suit for news interviews and such. Come to think of it, I haven't seen anyone like that for a while.'

'Nice cover, Alicia,' Trudy laughed, 'so glad you could get yourself out of that hole.'

'But we don't need to wear such high heels. We can look good and still be able to walk,' said Misaki, sticking to the subject, 'I wonder what she wears in the lab.'

'I think it's amazing that we are even talking about this,' I waved towards a group of guys grabbing themselves extra muffins, 'look at Robbie in his daggy shorts and t-shirt. Doesn't bother him a bit.'

'Oh the trials of being a female scientist,' said Trudy and we all agreed.

So it was possible that something was going on between Lisa and Conneally. Misaki had thought so. And if Brasindon was telling the truth, Conneally's death was more of an inconvenience for him than a triumph, there wasn't as much motive there as I had thought. If you really thought about it, Brasindon and Conneally were separated by the entire length of the VIP table. It would have been very difficult for Brasindon to get anything on to Conneally's plate without someone noticing. Conneally's wife, however, was sitting right next to him as he flirted with all the students flocking around the table. It might have been all too much, and it would have been so easy for her to poison the food.

If Nate looked into this at all, it was possible I had sent him in the wrong direction. This line of inquiry had reached a dead end. I needed to change my investigation and look into the possibility of an affair.

I realised that I would need to get moving. If I was going to talk with anyone from the conference I had to track them down before they left the state and went back home. It was a good thing that it was a weekend – I hoped that people had taken the chance to look around a bit before leaving.

So where were people likely to be on a Saturday? Well, there was only one place any self-respecting tourist would be on a sunny Saturday in Hobart – that would be the Salamanca Market. That was an easy answer to all of my problems. All I had to do was wander down to Salamanca Place and bump into people. And I might even pick up something nice while I was there – or at the very least, eat some olliebollen. Sometimes multi-tasking was just too much fun.

I walked from the café down into the market, enjoying the view of the crowds milling around and the multi coloured umbrellas on the stalls contrasting with the lovely old sandstone buildings on one side and the fresh greenery on the avenue of trees on the other. Then there was the view of the wharf, the old-fashioned tall ships with their masts sticking up higher than the wharf buildings. The smell of cooking from the food vans mingled with the smell of salt water. The sound of conversation mingled with the music from the various buskers, wafting, now louder, now softer on the breeze. Occasionally I could even hear the bagpipes warming up in the park before their weekly concert.

There are some days when I am totally sure that I live in the most beautiful place in the world. Today was without doubt one of those days. The crisp, clean air almost sparkled in the sunlight and you could feel the warmth of summer on the way. I moved into the market and made my way to the olliebollen stall. These Dutch donuts, fruity dough balls deep-fried and coated in icing sugar, always reminded me of my childhood. They were the staple food of the Olliebollen Festival – my school fair. Back then they were a treat that we partook of once a year, and as I savoured the sweet doughy goodness, I figured they should definitely remain a 'sometimes food'.

I walked past the stalls of knitted goods, children's handmade toys, pottery, and sweet smelling Huon pine woodwork. I enjoyed watching the people as much as checking out the goods. After all, I wasn't actually there to buy anything.

There was one stall where I had hoped to spend very little time. But as these things often happen, there was Robbie, right at the one place I wanted to avoid, and he was enthralled.

'How can you stand this place?' I asked by way of a greeting.

'Oh hi. The spiders? Isn't it brilliant. Look at that huge one there.'

These stall holders made their money by catching spiders, scorpions, and other bugs and encasing them in a glow-in-the-dark polymer. There were gearstick knobs containing scorpions, computer mice with larger arachnids encased within them, and then huge huntsman spiders and wolf spiders framed and ready to hang on your wall. Can you imagine having a plate-sized spider framed and hanging on your lounge room wall? Who would do that? Why would you want to? Around the outside of the tent were ropes hung with smaller arachnids encased in bracelets and necklaces ... It made my blood run cold.

'No. Brilliant is not how I'd describe this place. Not my cup of tea.'

'I've just bought two bracelets for my nieces back home. They'll freak out. It's going to be a fun Christmas this year. I would love to buy that big one there but I really don't have room in my luggage. It's a shame.'

'Can't see it. Honestly? It's so gross, I feel sick just being here. Do you have your bracelets yet? Can we move on?'

'They're just wrapping them now. I could stay here all day, but I guess there's more to see.'

'Sure is. And all of it better than this stall, if you ask me.'

We wandered through the market together. I was glad it was Robbie that I had run into. I wanted to check on him after Thursday night. Robbie usually kept his soul nicely tucked inside him under so many layers that a stranger might think he didn't have a soul at all. But on Thursday I had been able to see the pain in his eyes, and it was a big worry. However, now it looked like Robbie's soul was nicely tucked back away inside where it wouldn't bother others, and probably wouldn't bother him either. He didn't seem to be suffering any grief or remorse from the death of Conneally at all. I'm not sure, thinking about it, whether that was a better state of affairs as far as Robbie's total wellbeing went, but it was more normal.

'How are you feeling after, you know, the last week?' I asked.

'Bit of a different kind of conference, wasn't it? There was something up that night, not natural at all.'

That was interesting. Robbie thought that the death was strange too. Or he was just trying to look important. I am never sure with Robbie.

I tried to figure out a way to ask what I wanted to know without looking too forward. But I couldn't, so I just came straight out and asked.

'Do you think that Prof Conneally was having an affair?'

'Seriously? Who would he be having an affair with?'

'Well, perhaps Lisa?'

Robbie scoffed, 'Who has been saying that BS? That's daft.'

'She's a good looking girl, and you have to admit, she dresses to impress ...'

'Nah, that's just normal if you don't come from a backwater like this.' I reminded myself not to take offence – you just couldn't when it came to Robbie, you had to let it go. 'She's not anything out of the ordinary if you ask me. And Conneally is far too busy to have time to do anything like that. His wife was always at the conferences with him, always came to the dinners with him. Nope, just can't see it, myself. Total crap.'

I tell you what, this detective business is not good for the self-esteem. But I hid my disappointment. After all, Robbie was just a bloke. He might have missed the signals. I would try to find Lisa herself and see how she was. If she was having an affair then her grief should be obvious. There were always other avenues for investigation.

Robbie and I wandered through the market. He explained to me all the great places I should go and visit in Hobart, all the excellent things there were to do. I nearly reminded him that I lived here, and that I had originally told him about some of these places, but then I decided that it wasn't worth it. I half tuned him out and enjoyed the atmosphere of the market.

'Hey, do you want to join us for lunch?' Robbie asked, 'We're meeting at that great fish place on the wharf, just a group of us. It's a brilliant place – the fish is so fresh, caught on the day it's served.'

I tried to think. Next on my agenda was finding Lisa, but I had no idea whether she was still in the state. Maybe someone at the lunch would know where she was. And this way I could get some idea of what other conference attendees were thinking. And, well ...

'That sounds great,' I said, 'who wouldn't want to be near the water on a beautiful day like this?'

'It's near the whisky distillery too,' Robbie said with a grin, 'that's the afternoon's entertainment – whisky tasting. It's not a bad place here, really.'

'Oh, so glad it meets your high standards,' I gave the words a sarcastic twist. 'I think it's alright too, it's only my childhood home. Who is coming for lunch?'

'I have no idea – no-one is really organising it, it's just happening. My group will be there but I don't know who else. I mean, they don't know you're coming either.'

'True, sometimes the best things happen like that.'

It all sounded really delightful – lunch by the water, whisky tasting, friends and company. I decided to relax and enjoy the afternoon. If I caught up with some more people and found out more pertaining to the case, then well and good. If not, at least I would have had a fun afternoon, and that wasn't necessarily a bad thing. And I would be making more connections, which was necessary now that my big one, my big chance at Cambridge was gone. Maybe there would be someone there that would have a position for me. Why had I put all my eggs in the one basket? After Conneally's offer I had just stopped trying. Which, as it turned out, was a daft thing to do. Maybe today I could make it good again.

The seafood restaurant was pretty busy when we got there but there was a table outside being held by a few of the guys and the number of people sitting there was increasing all the time as more conference delegates happened to walk past and get stuck in conversation, or just turned up like I had following an impromptu invitation to lunch. It looked like three or four people had decided to meet for lunch and then each of them had invited another three or four.

At one end of the long wooden table, was Professor Geoffrey Gray. He was my supervisor at my last job, the job I left unexpectedly and abruptly to go and attend my mum in her illness. He was the ideal person to talk to about another academic position now that the Conneally job had fallen through. He might have another place for me in his group, or at least have ideas as to where I should try next. That would be the place to sit for lunch to get closer to my goal of getting a job.

At the other end of the table was Lisa, and to my eye she looked a bit upset. Sitting next to her would get me closer to finding out who had killed Conneally.

I knew where the sensible place to sit was but instead I followed my heart and pushed my way through the crowd to Lisa, greeting Geoffrey on the way but moving ever closer to my intended target.

'Lisa, how are you going? It must have been a very hard couple of days for you ...'

'It's been awful,' Lisa wailed and yes, my heart beat a bit faster.

'Were you very close to Prof Conneally?' I said in my most comforting, come to mamma, lay out all your troubles, voice.

'No, not especially,' not what I expected to hear, my inner triumph turned to confusion. 'I mean we work more with the postdocs than with the professors – it's a large research group. I would count myself lucky if he would talk to me about my work one time in a month.'

'Right ... so why has it been so awful?'

'The problem is, I'm two and a half years through my PhD, so close to the finish and now I have no idea what will happen. Can I still finish without a supervisor? And I was hoping that he would recommend me to some potential supervisors for a post-doctoral position but now he can't. What do I do now? How will I get people to notice me?'

Wow. This was not the grieving lover that I expected. I was stunned by her take on the situation. Did no-one else exist in the world? Did the world really revolve around her? She had not thought at all of Mrs Conneally, she wasn't even worried about the other students in her 'large research group'. I adjusted my tone to sound more like an advisory colleague than a comforting aunt.

'Yeah, it's a strange situation. It's not normal for someone to pass away suddenly like this. I'm sure someone can work it out for you though.'

'Oh I really hope so. I can't stop thinking about it.'

'Have you talked to any of the other professors at the conference?'

'Well, Professor Brasindon did come to see my poster. We had quite a long talk about my work, actually. Maybe I'll try to contact him.'

'I'd wait a little while though.'

'Really?' it took a little while for her to grasp that it might be insensitive to immediately go supervisor shopping a couple of days after your own has suddenly died but eventually she came around.

'It might be too soon, I guess I can email when I get back home.'

Grateful that Lisa could see a little of someone else's point of view, I tuned out the chatter of the happy group at the table and tried to get over my disappointment. It was pretty obvious that Lisa wasn't having any kind of relationship with Professor Conneally – let alone a romantic one. And wasn't it amazing how people could get on with their own little lives, caring so little for those around them? I didn't want everyone to be prostrated with grief for months, but this happy chatter was so out of tune with what just happened the other day. People were incredible in their ability to box things – to not let one thing spill into the next. Looking at the crew at the table you would think that they were all here on holidays, for the express purpose of enjoying themselves.

And so they were, I reminded myself. They were done with the conference and did not know the professor more than slightly. They didn't need to solve the murder, they didn't even think there was one. They were just making the most of a sunny day in a beautiful city.

But I felt differently. Whether it was my place or not, I had taken on some responsibility for finding the perpetrator of this murder and I wasn't on holiday. I needed to keep working on solving the murder, which probably meant no whiskey tasting today. But I would finish my lunch and keep digging and see what information I could get out of this group – I had focussed on Lisa as the possible mistress in an affair situation. Was there someone else? Could this still be a possibility?

The best person to get this information from would be Mrs Conneally. I was sure that the police would have had a conversation with her, and I could have gone crawling back to Jan and Nate again, but I was sure that Nate wouldn't tell me anything. And I didn't really want to reinforce their thinking that I'm a lunatic with one idea stuck in my head. No, there had to be another way.

I stole a potato chip from my neighbour and entered back into the friendly conversation but the problem kept playing over in the back of my head.

When I got home that night and wrote in my journal, I really had to laugh at myself. Was I really thinking that Lisa would break down during a very public lunch? That she would be all 'I'm so heartbroken, I don't care who knows anymore, I just lost my lover and I want to tell the world'. And instead she's all 'Man, someone has died and it has really stuffed my career. What am I going to do now to get things back on track. How inconvenient.' And she was so open about it, and not thinking at all about Professor Conneally's wife or the fact that he might have other friends and family.

But we don't really see much of that, do we? When we look at professors all we see is the research they are doing. When we think about professors it's only in relation to their work, we don't expect any personal life at all. And they feed that feeling. Some of them work 80 hour weeks, most work over 60 hours, they take work home, they work weekends.

So many marriages fall apart because the husband is all about the job. (I don't know whether female professors are also this one-eyed. I honestly don't know that many female professors.)

And the huge work load is actively encouraged by the universities – do more research, get more funding, publish more papers, and then you'll 'make it'. Well Conneally made it, I guess. He was looked up to and admired by everyone at that conference. But where has it got him? Dead.

If it was work-induced stress that killed him, that's bad enough. If it was work-induced murder, then that's really making a statement. Is the work worth it?

How did Mrs Conneally feel about all that work? Even if there was no affair, surely you would feel jealous coming second to a career? Mrs Brasindon seemed to see herself as part of her husband's success. His rewards were her rewards. Her personality swallowed into his. Is that a good thing? Is that what we can hope for? What happens to Mrs Brasindon when her 'kind, good, and generous husband' passes away? Will she actually become a personality then?

Somehow I needed to find Mrs Conneally, and carefully, gently, ask her some of my questions.

Sunday morning rolled around as it always does. And, as I always do, I got up and dressed and headed to church. I usually attend a church nearby full of young families and fun music, but this morning I felt the need for stability, the need to be part of an old fashioned service, so I headed into Hobart to the cathedral. I love the old words of the liturgy, words that have been said week upon week, for centuries. In the major changes of life, it is helpful to know that there are some constants. And it makes me feel close to Mum when I think of her saying the same words, singing the same hymns.

I guess Mrs Conneally felt the same way about the service, or maybe (if she indeed was the murderer) she thought that being at church was a great way to get rid of her guilt, because to my great surprise, when I settled myself in my pew and looked around, there she was. It took a lot of effort to concentrate on the service knowing she was there – two pews up, just out of my reach. Actually, once I saw her I didn't concentrate at all. I spent the whole sermon preparing what I was going to say to her afterwards. Rehearsing all my questions and her possible reactions.

I tell you something, she looked a right mess. Her hair looked like something the cat had dragged through the hedge backwards, her beige cardigan was pulled all wrong, and the tag was sticking up at the back. It drove me crazy looking at that all through the service and not being able to tuck it back in.

She cried to a greater or lesser extent for the whole of the service, pulling her hanky out of her sleeve and tucking it back in, over and over again. I wondered if I should go and sit with her and give her some comfort, but that didn't feel consistent with what I was intending to pry out of her afterwards, so I just let her be.

At the end of the service I hung around, waiting for her to get out of her seat to leave. She took a long time, just sitting there. Maybe she was praying, maybe she was just trying to stop crying. But eventually she stood up and I approached her and introduced myself.

'You don't know me, but I was at the conference with your husband and I just want to say how sorry I am for your loss.'

She immediately gave me a big hug (only slightly awkward, no, I'm lying, totally awkward) and said how grateful she was for my kind thoughts. And then she started crying again.

She didn't need any of my carefully prepared questions. It was like she was just busting to talk, she needed an outlet, she was just waiting for anyone to show the slightest interest in her and she would then overflow. She went on and on about how this trip had been so special because she was seeing where Alwyn had started his career.

I had to think hard at that point, who was Alwyn? But then I realised, he had always been

Professor A. Conneally, never a mention of his first name, and if his name was Alwyn I could understand why he wanted to hide it. It didn't suit him at all.

While I had been thinking that through Mrs Conneally had kept going. She said they had been going to head back to England via Townsville (Alwyn's birth place) and then next year the plan had been to visit Wales and see all her special places (she had been born in Wales, you see).

It was a tap I couldn't turn off. She told me all about their tourist adventures in Tasmania – Richmond (feeding the ducks and that gorgeous bridge), and Port Arthur (made her blood run cold but he had thought it was all so fascinating – he was curious, always curious), and Mt Field (such a funny name – is it a mountain or a field? But the waterfall was beautiful) and so on. She told me how devastated their friends would be and how she wished they had had children but they only had each other. She didn't know what was going to happen to her now and she had nothing left in her life. But she was so grateful for this little space of holiday that they had been given – it was like a second honeymoon, she said, just him and her and no work, just for a few days, so beautiful.

If she had committed murder then all I can say is that she is a consummate actor. I don't know what she was like before and it's just barely conceivable that this was all an act put on to throw people off the scent. But the thing is, no-one (but me) thinks this is murder. If she had done it, she wouldn't be thinking she had to throw anyone off the scent yet. No, I came away from that conversation convinced that she was a devastated widow.

I felt so sorry for her. And, to be honest, a bit stuck.

At home that afternoon I sat down with pen and paper to get my thoughts clear. I wrote a list to clarify where I was up to. I love lists, they make life so clear.

Prof Brasindon – no motive

Mrs Brasindon – possible motive but she would leave action to her husband, surely.

Mrs Conneally – no affair means no motive

Lisa – no affair and no motive

Some list, huh. It definitely clarified where I was up to. No suspects, no motives, no evidence of any kind. Nate and Jan were right, I was just going on a hunch and there was nothing to it. What was wrong with me?

It was clear, so clear, that there was nothing to this at all. My hatred for Brasindon had got in the way. My prejudice against well dressed women (who even knew I had that prejudice?) was blinding me. My grief was making my imagination run wild.

I closed the notebook and put on the TV. Tomorrow I would change projects. I would focus on getting myself a job. I would email Professor Gray and anyone else I could think of who could possibly offer me a position. I was done with this project. Oh, and tomorrow I would go crawling back to Nate and Jan and ask for their forgiveness and try to be friends again.

I was pulled out of a deep sleep the next morning by a strange sound. It wasn't an alarm – no work usually means no need for an alarm. It wasn't the rubbish truck. My sleepy brain was confused.

Eventually, and fortunately not too late, I realised it was my phone. Someone was actually calling me. Not a common occurrence anymore. I pulled myself together and hoped that I didn't still sound half asleep.

'Hello, Alicia speaking.'

'Alicia, are you interested in doing some analysis for me?'

It was Dr Susannah Pinkney from the Chemistry Department at the local university.

Susannah had been my supervisor when I'd completed my honours year. She had been the one to start me off on this research career.

When I had decided to go back to work, Susannah was the one I had called on first. It had been sensible to look for work locally, if I could work in Tasmania then my accommodation would be taken care of and, you know, I like the place.

So a month or so ago I'd printed out a resume and cover letter and decided to head in in person and take my chances – starting with Susannah.

I'd walked past the laboratory where I had spent my honours year working in Susannah's group. The lab where I had taken part in chemistry research for the first time, working over the summer break. I remembered how amazing it had felt to don the white coat and safety glasses and to break the ground on a new project, something that hadn't been done before, something that was important – that would last after I was gone. That was the point of working in science – to do something helpful for mankind. 'No matter how incrementally small the effect is,' said the cynical voice in my brain. It was true, ten years into my career I wasn't feeling like I had changed the world much. There had been no radical breakthrough, no amazing discovery, no Nobel prize. I had just added slowly and surely to the knowledge-base. But that was worthwhile, wasn't it?

Wasn't it?

On this day it felt like the researchers at this lab thought it was worthwhile. The lab was humming. White-coated bespectacled students were watching bubbling reactions, or passing solutions through silica-packed columns. The washing up racks were full of glassware and both rotary evaporators were going full pelt removing the solvent from newly formed products. It looked like Susannah's research group (and therefore her career) was reaching new heights.

I took a deep breath and knocked on the office door.

'Come' came the curt instruction, and I followed suit.

Susannah's desk was covered with printed journal articles, old exam papers, piles of textbooks, instrument read-outs and empty coffee cups. Red pen in hand she looked up at me over a paper she was filling with a scrawl of red marks and comments. I wondered who the unlucky student was and how much they would have to do to get it right.

'Hello? Oh hello Alicia, what are you doing here?'

'Oh good, you remember me.'

'Of course I remember you. Summer work and honours years are not that easily forgotten. How are you? What are you up to now?'

'Well, that's a bit of a long story. Do you have a few minutes?'

Susannah put down the page and turned to face me properly.

'Sure. Have a seat.'

I pulled out the seat and found it was covered with yet more paperwork. I picked up the stack, looked for somewhere to put it, and at Susannah's suggestion, piled it onto an already precarious pile of paper on the desk.

'I really must get to that. Now, tell me what's going on.'

'I actually came to ask a favour. And it's a bit of a big one. I've been working on the mainland – a post-doc for Prof Lefky, and one for Jamie Sorenson (you know him, right?) and a few other things. But then, well ...'

I stopped then, and took a deep breath. I had known that I would need to tell Susannah the story, but I just hadn't realised how hard it would be.

'You know how it has always been just Mum and me? Well, Mum got sick. Pancreatic cancer. So I dropped everything and came home.'

'Oh Alicia. Oh I'm so sorry. How is she now?'

I shook my head. I had thought I would be able to say it but the words stuck in my throat. And Susannah understood.

'That's very hard. How long ago?' Susannah reached over the desk and put her hand on my arm.

'It's been a few months. I've been, well, it's been ...'

'Of course.'

I wiped my eyes and tried to pull myself together. How did I not see that I would have to go through this? Or maybe that's why I had put off the return to work.

'I don't want pity, or to put you under pressure, but I was wondering if there was any work going here? I'm happy to do some research assistant work or something casual but I have to get back into it again, and I can't quite leave Tassie yet.'

Susannah nodded.

'I'd love to help you out, but I don't really know what I can do. You know that money's always tight.'

Yes, I knew that full well. There is never enough money, never any spare. I wondered if I was asking the impossible. But then, if you don't ask ...

'What sort of research have you been doing lately? Maybe we can find somewhere that you will fit.'

We cleared a space on the desk (yet more piles of paper) and wrote notes and drew diagrams, sharing her research and mine. Susannah had called in her students to explain aspects of their work or to describe their latest dilemma. Talking science again was invigorating and I felt like I had jumped back into the pool and immediately remembered how to swim and just how good the water felt.

'Maybe you could give a seminar Alicia, although it's really the wrong time of year for that. Everyone is going to conferences or on leave right now. If you can wait until February we might be able to set one up for you.'

'That would be great, thanks,' I said but my heart sank. February! It was only mid-November. February was so far away. Things really didn't happen quickly in the university setting.

It had been a great talk, good for the brain, good for the self-esteem, but unfortunately not so good for getting me immediate employment.

But Susannah had been helpful in every way that she could. It was she who had managed to get me a registration for the conference in December. She had been truly fantastic and I felt a bit guilty for not making more of the opportunity job-wise by talking more with prospective employers at the conference.

And here she was, helping me out again.

'This really needs to be done asap. It's government work, mass spectrometry. Eoin would do it usually but he's on leave right now – out of the country as far as I know. And I thought of you because of your CV.

You can do mass spec. Right? And NMR if we need it?'

'Sure can. It might take me a little while to orient myself to the instrument but it should be fine.'

'Right, well, I'll give you more information when you get in, but if we could see you first thing this morning that would be great. You didn't have other plans did you? This is pretty urgent.'

Apart from investigating a murder? Unofficially investigating a murder? Getting nowhere fast with trying to investigate something that possibly wasn't murder?

'No, not really.' It would be much nicer to do some work and get some income and feel like I was helping someone out.

I pulled on jeans and a shirt and made sure that I was wearing shoes that covered my feet completely. It had been a while since I had been in the lab. I did a quick search of the obvious places in the cottage but couldn't find my favourite safety glasses. I would have to make do with whatever scratched and uncomfortable pair the university was happy to lend me. Ah well.

I had work. That was good news. Even if it was just a little bit of work. I wanted to tell someone. I wanted (to be honest) to tell Mum. So who else could I tell? Who else cared and knew where I was at and would be happy for me?

Well, Jan, of course. But we hadn't parted on the best of terms.

At least, I hadn't parted with her on the best of terms. Did she even know I was upset with her? Obviously she'd know by the way I'd stormed out last time we met that I was upset, but upset with her? Maybe not. Maybe if I just … if I just went into The Lemon Tree and ordered a coffee. I could see how she felt about me by her reaction and then I could let her know the good news.

There was no-one else that I could just talk to like Jan. Trudy would be asking about future plans, about how this would help my career. Jan would just listen and be excited for me.

Trudy would be too busy to chat to me before work anyway. No, Jan was it. I'd give it a go.

'Alicia! Hey, great to see you.'

Well, that was kinda nice. A nice greeting. Maybe she didn't think I was upset with her.

'Hi Jan, how's it going?'

'Want the usual?'

'Yes, but to take away thanks. I have work at the uni today.'

'You have work? That's awesome. Well done.' Jan turned the handle on the steamer and got to work on my coffee straight away.

'Thanks.' I moved towards the coffee machine so we could keep chatting.

'What kind of work?'

'Analysis of some sort. Not really sure actually, I only know that it has to be done asap. I know I'll be doing Mass spec though. And maybe NMR.'

'Oh. Good. You know those terms mean nothing to me.'

'It's this analysis where, hmmm, how do I explain it in thirty seconds?'

'How about you drop around at the end of the day, tell me how your first day back at work went, and explain it to me then?'

'That would be brilliant. I'm sure I'm going to need someone to debrief with. Thanks Jan, if you're sure?'

'Of course I'm sure. I wouldn't have asked if I wasn't. And I'm going to be curious all day, so make sure you come.'

It was so nice. Nice to be friends with Jan again. Great to feel like we were connecting. Maybe I'd read too much into everything before. Maybe she didn't think I was insane after all. Or maybe she was just happy that I'd changed the subject. I didn't know, but I really liked the idea of chatting to someone about the first day back, having someone to debrief with. I was sure there would be a lot to say.

I parked my car a couple of blocks away from the university like I had always done as a student. I had always been too poor to pay for the little parking there was available on campus – and old habits die hard. Walking my regular route, my memories of student life came back to me. There, on my left, was the law school. I remembered being able to tell which students were law students. They were always dressed smartly and the girls carried tiny handbags. They had to dress as if they were going into a courtroom I had been told, and the dress sense set them apart.

Arts students were dressed in a much more avant garde fashion. They were the girls with the green hair, the flowing dresses and Doc Marten boots. Or the boys dressed in long trench coats and top hats.

The science students tended to wear jeans and clever t-shirts with slogans like '2 + 2 = 5, for extremely large values of 2' or 'Obey gravity! It's the Law!' which they apparently thought funny (I still think they are funny, but I'm a geek). But the real way to tell a science student was by the large backpack they were dragging around, filled with notes and textbooks.

Walking up the hill past the engineering school to the chemistry building with the big smoke stacks sticking out of the roof took me right back to my undergrad days. My years of earning an income and making my own way in the big city faded to almost nothing. It was hard to believe that over ten years had passed since I was taking down notes in uncomfortable chairs in large lecture theatres, running up to the laboratories on top of the hill to make it on time for my biochemistry labs, or eating sandwiches with my friends on the lawns in the sunshine.

But now here I was, an adult, a scientist, a researcher, and I needed to know that again. Needed to know who I was again. Needed to be with my people, my tribe, other scientists.

'Thanks so much for this Susannah. I don't want to sound over the top but it's great to be doing some paid work again.'

'No, you're really helping us out. With Eoin on holidays, and the coroner asking for a quick result, it was great to have you on tap, as it were.'

'Hang on, the coroner?'

'Yes, oh yes, I haven't really told you yet, have I? How about you close the door just for a second.'

This sounded serious. Closing the door for privacy had happened maybe twice in my whole university career. My curiosity was well and truly piqued.

'The situation, as I understand it, is that someone has died, and when the post-mortem was done there was no obvious cause for the death. No evidence of heart attack or aneurism or anything. The pathologist has sent us a saliva sample and the police found a glass vial that we're hoping to get information from. They are both in the fridge in the lab. I'll get them for you in a second. There's only a few milligrams of sample so it's not going to be an easy analysis but if you could just do your best that would be great.'

'This wouldn't be related to Professor Conneally's death, would it?' I had to ask.

'Officially? I can't say.'

'Unofficially?'

Susannah gave the slightest of nods.

I felt an unholy glee spread through me. It was murder. I knew it.

Before you ask, I didn't give a big whoop and dance around the office. I kept my face straight – it wouldn't do to show unsightly enthusiasm. A man had died, had been killed, this was serious business. But still, the sense of vindication was brilliant.

I got myself under control and put my professional mask firmly in place.

'So I'll be doing Mass Spec. And NMR? Would you be able to remind me where the instrument lab is? Nothing much has changed, I'm supposing, since I was here last?'

'It's pretty much the same, I'm sure. And I've booked the NMR for you for the next couple of days. There really is very little sample. You may need an overnight just to get a carbon, the NOESY and COSY will take ages. And that's assuming it's fairly pure. See how you go.'

'Sure, I'll do my best. The other thing I need is some lab glasses. Is that ok?'

'Sure, I'll just get our lab tech to get you some. His name's Joshua – did you meet him before? You probably should get to know him at some stage.' Susannah opened the door and called into the lab but there was no response.

'Great. He should be here, but he's been so unreliable lately,' she complained, 'not sure what's got into him. I guess I'll take you down to the store myself.'

'Maybe he's wanting to move on from being a lab tech.'

'Well if he's wanting to move on to research, he's going the wrong way about it, that's all I can say. I wouldn't recommend him to any future employer at the moment. He's never been awesome, but this last week he's been atrocious.'

'People are strange.'

'You can say that again.'

All kitted out with new safety glasses and a pristine white lab coat for good measure, I made my way with the samples to the instrument lab and fired up the mass spectrometer. It had been a while since I had used one but it all looked very familiar and I found myself feeling very much at home. I waited for the instrument to equilibrate, diluted and prepared the samples, and hummed a contented tune.

A fresh-faced student stuck his head in the door at around 11am and invited me to morning tea. So that tradition was still happening. That was good really. Staff and students gathering around one table in the tearoom and talking about nothing in particular. I was happy to have a break and join in. I thought I might even be able to make a few more connections. Maybe one of the other staff in the department would have a position going soon.

I found an unused cup in the back of a high cupboard, and made myself a black tea. Tea bags were provided, but milk was always in short supply no matter which university. I learned to drink tea black a long time ago.

There weren't a lot of people in the room – quite a few had taken Christmas holidays early, or as Susannah had said, were at conferences. The undergraduate year had ended and there was a festive feel. Someone had brought in a cake. For no reason – they just felt like baking. It was all very pleasant.

Susannah introduced me to each of the people sitting at the table, staff to my right, and students gathered to my left, and I tried to remember all the names. Susannah immediately got caught in an intense conversation with other staff about the requirements of the coding of the staff credit cards. Important conversation for sure, but it wasn't giving me an opportunity to showcase my skills as a researcher and after listening to talk of scanning receipts and taking photos with smart phones to upload to specific software, I thought the conversation might be at least a little more interesting in the other direction.

'Now, what were your names again?' I asked the student sitting next to me.

'I'm Dan, and this is Liv,' he said gesturing to the girl sitting opposite him, 'we work with Susannah on natural products.'

Trim and neat, her black hair braided neatly, Liv was dressed in what I like to call 'lab chic' – all sweet and girly, nice floral skirts and pretty t-shirts, matched with great big boots to get around the 'shoes must cover the whole foot' rule. Dan, with his blonde artfully-styled hair, green sweater and jeans, looked like a poster boy for an American business college.

'And are you finishing up soon Dan?' it was as good a place as any to start with a PhD student.

'Yep. Well, I hope so. Sometimes it feels like I'll never finish.'

'I remember that feeling well.'

'Every time I think I'm done, Susannah sends me back to the lab for more experiments. I'm hoping I'm close to the end.'

'You know Dan, it's your thesis. You decide in the end whether you're done or not.' Why did these students make me feel like the elderly maiden aunt?

'Yeah,' Dan took a sip of his coffee, 'I guess so.' He didn't sound too convinced.

'You should definitely take advice from Susannah, I'm not saying that you shouldn't do that. But you can't keep going forever.'

'I know, it's sort of safe to keep going though, I'm really not sure what I'll do after this. This is ... kinda easy. I mean, the work's not easy, but at least I know what I'm doing here.'

'Why did you choose to do a PhD? Did you want to go into research?'

'Oh ... I just ... I finished high school and then uni was easy to get into (easier than finding a job) and then honours and then ... well ... the scholarship was easy to get too, and here I am. I'm not sure what I want to do next. Probably post-doc somewhere.'

'Do you want to travel? Do you have some-where in mind?'

'That's the problem. I know I could go, but my girlfriend is here, and she doesn't want to leave – she has a job here. It's all feeling pretty complicated, you know?'

'So you're putting off the decision by not finishing.'

'Touché! I don't know. I have to finish, I know ...'

'I hope it goes well for you, whatever you decide to do. I can see how hard it is though. Where are you at Liv?'

'Oh I'm just in my second year. I think it's going ok, but I have so much to do. I feel like I'll never hand my thesis in. I had a talk for the conference, so that's just taken up all my time for the last couple of months. Or at least it feels like it.'

'A talk as a second year, that's pretty good. I only presented posters in my first and second years. Did you have a talk too Dan?'

'Yep, the two of us gave talks, the rest of the group had posters. And now I need to catch up on all the work I've missed. Speaking of which ...'

Dan finished off his coffee with one swig, and together the two of them said their good-byes and left the table.

'Well, that was an interesting conversation.' This comment came from the man sitting opposite me. I hadn't really looked at him before but now he caught my attention. He had long black hair tied back from his face with a rubber band, strands hanging out everywhere. He wore a grubby t-shirt and his pants had holes in them and I would put good money on his shoes being the cheapest you could buy from K-Mart. I was sure I recognised him from somewhere.

'I'll tell you something for nothing. They need to put a rocket up Dan, he's been here way too long. If you ask me, he shouldn't even be here. If he doesn't pull his finger out he's going to be chucked out of the uni. The Dean and that, they only let you have so long. I dunno what he thinks will get him through. If he tried to get a job anywhere they wouldn't take him on.

'I had to work 60 hour weeks during under-grad. Forty contact hours at uni and another twenty at the shop to get money to live off and I didn't complain. He's just had it too easy. No idea what work is.'

The guy had decided that I needed to know his opinion about everything in the research group. He obviously didn't want me to have too high an opinion of the students I had been talking to. I wasn't sure what to say in response but it turned out I didn't need to say anything, the grumbling continued in a steady stream without any encouragement needed.

'And Liv, Liv doesn't think for herself, ever. She's not even really doing her own research, she only does what Susannah tells her to do. And Susannah lets her do it. She should be made to think for herself for a while. Otherwise, what's the PhD worth? She honestly doesn't know a thing about what she's doing. You should hear her in group meeting.

'And don't even get me started about the state of the lab. No-one cares if the glassware is clean. No-one ever puts anything away. And you'd think they'd take some responsibility for the dry solvents or the ordering but no, they just leave it up to me. I tell you, I'm jack of it. I'm not their servant. I'm the lab technician. I should take a break and leave them to it. It would all fall over in pretty quick order I reckon.'

So this was Joshua the lab technician that Susannah was talking about earlier. I could see what Susannah was saying now. He looked as unreliable as they came in spite of what he was saying about being the linchpin of the research group. I wondered why Susannah was putting up with him and whether the university management structure just didn't allow anything to be done about it.

As soon as I could find a break in his unrelenting litany of complaint I made my excuses and got back down to the lab. Anything was better than listening to that. Sometimes I think that it's a shame that all jobs come with people attached.

As I walked back down the long hallway to the instrument room it clicked. I had seen him at the conference with that girl. He was the one that had been pointing something out at Brasindon's lecture. I almost turned around to ask him what was going on there but I decided I had better not. I didn't want to get him started again.

'So then she took me down this long dark hallway, right down in the basement of the building. And through a door with a keypad lock on it, and past a couple of offices and into the instrument room. It was like heading down into Dr Jekyll's laboratory or something. I truly wondered what would be at the other end.'

'But you're here to tell the tale. What a relief.'

I had finished up at the uni and headed back to The Lemon Tree to debrief. Jan had been true to her word – she really wanted to hear about my day. And I was happy to tell her. Telling a real human being was so different to just writing in your journal. Humans laugh (or groan) at your jokes. And this human gave you slices of carrot and ginger cake to nibble on while you were chatting. No such delicacies were available at my cottage.

'I know. I know. I'm such a dag.' Ok, so I was playing it up a bit. But truly, the hallway down to the instrument lab could be really spooky – especially if no-one had turned the lights on. You could almost hear the music playing.

The café was closed, we were sitting in the cosy apartment that Jan and Nate had carved out of the back rooms.

'So what were the things Susannah was showing you?'

'They are pretty big machines, but we don't call them machines – we call them instruments. I think because they do such delicate work. These were Mass Spectrometers. MS for short. They take unknown compounds, ionise them with electro-spray ionisation and measure the fragments to identify the compound. It's fascinating really. You take something completely new, something that someone has made in the lab. You inject the teeniest bit into this big instrument, bombard it with a chemical – a proton donor – until it blows apart. Then you capture the particles in the quadrupole ion trap and you measure the mass to charge ratio and by working backwards and maybe matching it to a library of compounds you can find out exactly what the new compound is.' I took a bite of the cake, so delicious.

'Right. Can I just pretend that made sense? It all sounds pretty complicated.'

'Ok, let's see. How do I make this simpler? We take chemicals that people have made in the lab and blow them to pieces in a controlled way in a big machine and then measure the pieces. Then we put the jigsaw back together and we know what we had to start off with.'

'Before you blew it up.' Jan didn't look so convinced.

'Right.'

'But if it's blown up, it's no use anymore, right?'

'Oh we only need a little bit, just a tiny fraction of a gram. The rest is fine to use. And sometimes (like what I'm doing right now) we just want to find out what the chemical is. We don't need to use it for anything.'

'And you can tell exactly what it is from that?' Jan waved towards the cake, offering me more. Why not? I had worked hard all day and this was a great reward.

'It helps if the researcher knows what they think they've made. So you know what you're looking for. The library of compounds helps with the identification too – comparing your results with previous results and putting all the puzzle pieces together. And there's a couple of other methods: NMR and IR that give you other pieces of information and if you put it all together you can solve the puzzle.'

'That makes a little more sense. So NMR?'

'That's, Nuclear Magnetic Resonance spectroscopy, oh boy, I guess you could say you look at the carbon and hydrogen atoms in the molecule and what sort of atoms and bonds are around them.' I tried to draw a molecule in the air with my hands .

'Right ...' Jan drew the word out, she didn't sound convinced, 'and, what was the other one? R something?'

'IR. Infrared Spectroscopy – you shine a light at the molecule and it makes it wiggle, you measure the wiggles and you can see what types of bonds or groups you have in the molecule.' This time my hands were the molecule showing the bending vibration and the twisting vibration, but it was no good.

'Oh my goodness. I have no idea what you're saying.' Jan laughed at me and at my waving hands, which had nearly waved the cake off the plate.

'Ha. Just believe me, I can take a compound, and with a bit of background information I can work out what it is. It's like those logic problems, you know? 'Mrs White lives in the house next door to the poodle and three along from the garden with the pink flowers'? I never do those, I usually get enough of it at work.'

'Sounds like it. So what have you found?'

'It's a bit tricky. The MS didn't match to anything in the library – not that I could see, but I'll have another look tomorrow. There were a few near misses but nothing concrete.'

'And the N, the other one, the carbon and hydrogen one?'

'The NMR. Well, the hydrogen by itself doesn't tell you too much, unless you know what you're looking for. And the carbon is still running. There was so little sample that it's going to take a long time. Maybe I'll get an answer, or part of an answer in another couple of days.'

'I hope it's not too frustrating for you. I'm glad you've got work. Are you enjoying it?'

'I am, it's so good to be back in the lab again. I thought I was ready to be back, but I didn't realise how ready I was.'

It was almost like the old days again. Jan and I, best friends again. Almost. You can see that I made no mention of what exactly I was doing. No mention of Conneally or that this was an investigation into the means of his murder. I mean, it was good to chat with Jan, but I knew if I had brought up the professor again that a barrier would have gone up between us. She probably thought I'd forgotten all about it in the excitement of work. I was happy for her to think that.

When the last crumbs of cake were eaten off my plate I grabbed my bag and said my goodbyes. It had been great to chat but I was also looking forward to some alone time. And I didn't really need to be there when Nate came home.

I wasn't sure, obviously, what Nate was thinking, but if the police had found a glass vial that they thought was connected to Conneally's death then he must know that the death was suspicious. He must have known for the whole weekend.

Even if he hadn't been put on the case himself, Hobart is a small place and he would have been keeping an eye out after our conversation. He must have known.

And yet he didn't tell me. He didn't come and talk to me about it. He didn't tell me that I had been on the right track.

Maybe he didn't even tell Jan.

If he had told Jan then I felt even worse. They both knew that I was interested, worried even, about this. And yet, it didn't occur to them to put me out of my misery and tell me that an investigation was ongoing? I could have been helpful to the investigation, I was being helpful to the investigation, but not through Nate. Not the way I thought I would.

I had matched the substance in the vial that was found in the bathroom to the saliva sample. They both had the same substance in them. But what that substance was, I didn't know yet. But I would. I would work it out.

However, if they were not telling me anything about their investigation, then I would not tell them anything about my own investigation and we'd see who worked it out first. It sounded fair to me.

I walked through the front door of my little cottage on the river and dropped my keys on the hall table. This place was unchanged since my childhood. I almost expected Mum to wander out of the kitchen, wiping her hands on a tea towel and telling me she had put the kettle on and that I was just in time for a cuppa.

But instead, I had to go in to the kitchen and put the kettle on myself. Which I did. Even though I'd just had a drink with Jan and didn't need any more liquid. Just the sound of the kettle, the feel of the warm cup in my hand, was comforting.

I have lived in quite a few different apartments over the last years. Different little homes in different cities. But none of them felt like home, not like this place did. This cottage was my anchor.

If I got work in another city I would probably have to sell the cottage, or at least rent it out. Could I bring myself to sell it? I looked around again. Would this place even sell? The kitchen was straight out of the seventies – orange bench top, brown floor tiles, wooden cupboard doors, a tiny little fridge. It worked as a food preparation area, but it wasn't beautiful. Not even slightly.

Warm cup in hand I wandered through the rest of the cottage, seeing it with new eyes. The dining room – pokey and dark. The long lounge room with the net curtains and the gold carpet and oh, yuk, the brown square patterns on the wallpaper. The brown carpet tiles in the hallway with yet another brown patterned wallpaper. The broken venetian blinds on the bedroom windows. It felt like home to me, but it looked dreadful from a buyer's perspective. Awful.

But the bare bones were good. Most of the problems were cosmetic. If I removed the wallpaper and painted, and put in new carpet, and maybe if I knocked a wall out between the lounge and dining room that would help it out. The afternoon sun coming in the lounge window would make it all the way through to the dining room wall in winter. It could be gorgeous.

The kitchen would need a complete work-over but I could do the painting and some of the knocking out myself and keep costs down that way. It could be a really fun project too. I could see myself now, renovator by day, writer of job applications by night. It was a thought.

I threw a frozen dinner in the microwave and sat down to eat it, putting the house renovations on the back burner and thinking again through the interesting development of the day. The murder investigation was back on. Conneally had been poisoned somehow with something. And I was able to use my chemistry skill to answer some questions. I was now officially on the case.

I wondered if Nate had brought Brasindon in for questioning following the one lead I had given in our conversation. I could imagine the scene – Nate and Brasindon facing off over a metal table in an interview room, recording device blinking its red light to show that every word is being kept for posterity (do they use tapes now, I wonder, or is it all through MP3 or something?) and Nate saying to Brasindon,

'I am sure, sir, that you can see that we have to look into every possibility.'

And Brasindon replying 'I don't see that at all. I don't know why you would even think that I have anything to do with this death.'

'It is common knowledge that your relationship with the deceased has been strained at times.' (Do you like that touch? 'The deceased'? I am so professional.)

'Again, I do not see that your question is of any significance. We are two professionals, working as professionals. I did not treat Professor Conneally any differently to the way I would treat anyone else.'

(Which is true, he treats everyone badly.)

And then Nate could have asked, 'Were you in competition for the same funding?'

And Brasindon would have told him about his research funding and how he now needs a new partner.

'Do you have any evidence of this situation?'

'It is in the public domain. You could have found that yourself if you had done even a little research.'

And then I guess Nate would be cursing me for throwing him off, but if he'd just talked to me I could have told him the same information with much less embarrassment.

I wondered if, just maybe, Brasindon had been in that very situation, in an interview with Nate or another police officer, on Saturday while I had been having morning tea with his wife. No wonder he was in such a foul mood when he came to pick her up. Had Nate dropped my name? Surely not.

Anyway, it looked like I would never know. Nate obviously wasn't going to tell me anything, and Professor Brasindon will never speak to me again if he can help it.

But I would continue my own investigation. I would take it more seriously now that

I knew for sure that Professor Conneally had been murdered.

Surely there was something in my memories that would help me point the finger at someone. I just needed to go back through the conference day by day and think about the behaviour of people. Something would give someone away, I was sure of it.

I decided to read through my journal and see whether I had inadvertently written myself some clues. Something that didn't seem important at the time but would be important now. It all felt incredibly Agatha Christie but hey, I knew that the murderer wasn't me, and I was the one that had been at the conference and met all the suspects. It was worth a try.

I flipped back through the pages – where to start reading?

I was going to start with the conference but something made me turn a few more pages back, and find a conversation I had forgotten about. The conversation with Trudy about a lecturer called Ken Jones.

I'd met up with Trudy for lunch on the day I'd gone to look for work. We had been friends since our undergraduate degree and I was always ready for a catch up with her – whenever time permitted, which was not often with Trudy.

'What do you think my chances are of getting work here in paradise?' I had asked raising my voice to be heard above the hubbub of voices and the background music in the university refectory.

'Well, you might be as lucky as me and get a three month contract but there's not much going.'

'A three month contract?'

'Yep. That's how it's been lately. Three month contract after three month contract but I've managed to stay on. You have to take what you're given when you're trying to stay in one place for your family.'

'I don't know whether to be impressed or horrified.'

'To be honest, neither do I. You never know, things might be better in Chemistry but in Biochem that's just how it is.'

'How are your family? The kids doing ok?'

'Thanks for asking,' she said cheekily, 'you know I try to pretend they don't exist when I come here. No, they are going well, it's easier now they are all in primary school, I just have all the running around to after school activities to do now. It's easier in the summer when the soccer season is over – four boys to four different soccer games each Saturday morning. It's a bit of a stretch.'

'I can imagine. No, I can't. I won't tell you about my Saturdays, you'll probably hit me.'

Trudy took a playful swipe at me anyway and made rude noises about the lazy life of the unemployed.

'I guess I should be apologising for taking you away from your work, then.'

'No, lately I've been making the effort to treat myself with a bit more care. I'm trying to give myself time to eat. I mean everyone deserves to taste the food they're eating, right?'

'Eating is one of the basic rights, yes. Haven't you been eating? I don't understand.'

'Oh, I've been eating, but I've eaten my lunch at my desk while I've been working. I've decided it's not good for me. I'm going to take the time to eat and actually taste the food.'

'Shows how long I've been away from the desk. I had forgotten those days eating 'al desco'. I remember a staff meeting where the boss said, 'I know you're all feeling under time pressure, but I've seen you going to the toilet. I only go to the toilet at lunch time.''

'Seriously? You weren't meant to use the toilet? We're not quite that bad here. Not yet.'

'You can use the loo, but you can't eat, is that it?'

'Pretty much. But I'm standing against the trend.'

'You rebel!'

'That's me.' Trudy picked up her toasted sandwich and bit with great relish.

I had told Trudy then the good news about getting a registration for the conference, and she had informed me about the excitement in the Biochemistry Department because Professor Conneally was coming to speak.

'Oh yes, the poster child for Tasmanian Biochemistry,' I said, 'is he well remembered up in Biochem?'

'He's definitely remembered. Some of us hate him more than others.'

'What? What's the story? Sounds totally juicy.'

Trudy looked at her sandwich in a contemplative manner.

'It was a little bit before my time, so all of my knowledge is second or third hand, but it sounds like Conneally's motto in life was 'You don't climb to the top of the ladder without stepping on a few heads' and there are people here who still feel the pain.'

'Such as?'

'Such as Ken Jones.'

'I think I remember him – he taught genetics, right? Short, stocky, greying hair like a wire brush sticking up?'

'Yes, that's him. Totally grey hair now. And he's still teaching genetics even now, lowly lecturer Dr Ken Jones, while Professor Conneally is up in Cambridge with the big boys.'

'But surely it's your quality of work that decides how far up the ladder you are?'

'Now you're being naive Alicia. There are so many ways that colleagues can boost a career or keep it low. Conneally would block Ken's in-house funding applications, deny him the money to pay for his work to be published in high ranking journals and so on. Conneally was held in high esteem by the university – he'd brought in a bit of money and the uni thought he was the bees knees, anything he said went and what he said boosted his own career at the expense of everyone else's.

'In fact, there's talk of one year where the Jones group had started to grow but he hadn't managed to get his hands on government funding yet. The story is that he was running out of money to do any research at all – he couldn't pay for animals to do experiments on, or reagents, or cell lines, or antibodies, or anything. He was in a bad way and he approached all the staff at a staff meeting to ask for support for a special funding application to keep his work going. But Conneally wouldn't hear of it. He said it would make the school look bad to be begging for cash. He didn't want that reputation. He thought it would adversely impact his own reputation. So he cut Ken off completely.

Ken's career would have been pretty much over if some of the other staff didn't take pity on him and lend him stuff. As it was he had to drop students and pretty much start his group from scratch when he managed to get funding again.'

'But Jones is still here,' I said.

'Yes, he's here but he's bitter. He's sure (and maybe he's right) that a little help from Conneally when he was starting out would have meant a good deal to his career. He's taken to wandering the corridors muttering, 'Who does he think he is, coming to lord it over us' and so on.'

'And there's me thinking the Biochemistry Department would be proud of their big export.'

'Human nature. And the tall poppy syndrome. Much more likely to tear someone down than build them up. It's sad but true.'

'And look at us, doing the same thing, passing on the terrible gossip.'

'You look really shaken by it Alicia.'

'Maybe I've been looking back at things through rose-coloured glasses. I've forgotten the pressure and the politics.'

I had forgotten somehow just what it was like at the uni, but Trudy had brought me back to earth with a bump. Was the pressure enough to bring someone to murder? I mean, we joke about it all the time – I could just kill him – but no one ever means it.

But someone had meant it this time. And it's the little things that give the game away.

I could start building my list again.

I had one suspect. Ken Jones.

He'd been at the conference and he held a grudge.

Actually, come to think of it, he was the one telling the heart attack story just before the dinner.

And when you thought about that, well, it got even more suspicious. Why did he bring up his heart attack? Was it just to get people thinking in the right way when Conneally died? No one else was sharing health stories, but he just happened to bring it up. I guess it backfired on him though – it was that very story and Conneally's response that made me think that this death was a murder in the first place.

Had he even been in Singapore? I guess that was a fact we could verify. I would have to look into Ken Jones a bit more. Maybe I'd have morning tea in the biochemistry building instead of the chemistry building. It was a bit of a trek up the hill but the results would be worth it.

I had a look through a few more pages of my journal and found the page where I wrote about all the people watching I had done in Brasindon's oh so incredibly boring lecture. And that brought up yet another suspect. It was amazing what you could find when you looked with the right attitude.

That crazy girl – headphones girl. Watching movies in the sessions, giving an unprepared and unsuccessful talk, and then, at the conference dinner, mooning over Professor Conneally like she was really impressed by him and everything chemistry. And I was sure she dropped something into his bag while she was with all the giggling girls at the dinner. Would it be possible for me to find out what that was that she had 'given' him? It was all very suspicious activity. (There I go, muttering into my beard. Not that I have a beard, but muttering, anyway. It was suspicious though.)

I thought about how I could find out more about her. She would be a lot harder to investigate than Jones. I didn't even know which university group she was in. Her accent was Australian but there were plenty of Australian universities represented at the conference and she could easily have been working in the US or the UK.

Then I remembered the abstracts book. I don't know how I could have forgotten it. I spent long enough packing the conference show bags.

Susannah had given me a ring the day before the conference started and asked if I could possibly help with the organisation. How could I say no? It was one way to pay her back for paying for the conference. I had intended to spend that Monday reading and researching and getting my head into the right work-space, but instead I spent it putting lanyards and name tags together, packing conference bags with flyers, notepads, pens, and a few mints, collecting boxes of wine for the welcome wine-taster and trying to make room in the staff fridge for the white and bubbly, all kinds of little fiddly jobs.

Just as we had it all together, Susannah had burst into the room looking more stressed than I had ever seen her.

'Where are all the abstracts?'

'They are in the bags, we've put one in each bag. Why?'

'I just got off the phone with those dimwits in New England, apparently two of their students have intellectual property issues with their talks and have to be pulled. Two talks! We're going to have to go through every book and rip out the abstracts.'

'Good thing they are spiral bound then. Will that change the program much?'

'No, they are going to present something, I managed to talk them into that. But just not what's been put into the book.'

'That's a bit of a relief. But why didn't they pick it up sooner?'

'That's what I'm asking. It's crazy. You don't prepare for a conference with stuff that has to be kept confidential. It's ridiculous. I can't tell you how frustrated I am.'

'Don't worry, we'll sort it.'

And we did. We opened every single bag, pulled out the abstracts book, ripped out (neatly) two pages from the middle for shredding, and put the book back into the bag like nothing had happened. It took a reasonable amount of time to doctor 400 bags or so. And I had developed a close and personal relationship with the abstracts book. Well, it was time to get to know it just that little bit better.

I pulled my copy from the conference out of the bag that I had flung on the floor next to the front door and had a look at the first couple of pages – they contained a headshot of all the participants and their contact details. The photos were pretty atrocious and I found it hard to recognise anyone for a while. People looked so different once they had been printed in black and white and shrunk to a thumbnail size. But I kept searching. Eventually I found the photo of headphones girl and I turned to the page indicated for the abstract of the talk. And there it wasn't. It was one of the talks we had pulled.

No wonder her talk was so bad, so unpre-pared and badly presented. She'd had about two days to write it, and she was only an honours student, only in her fourth year of an undergraduate degree. No wonder she was disinclined to pay attention after all the stress she must have had the few days leading up to the conference. What a disappointment. But motive for murder? Who knows?

If she was that upset from having her work pulled, why was she giggling and chatting at the conference dinner? Was she up there, trying to look natural, just so that she could put something in Conneally's food?

Well, there it was. I had my suspicions but I couldn't do anything about them. There was no way to casually investigate this girl like I could with the whole affair situation. There was not much chance of something seren-dipitous happening like with Mrs Conneally or Mrs Brasindon – I was pretty sure that everyone from outside of Tasmania would have gone home by now. No one had told them to hang around – no one thought it was murder until too late. What was I going to do?

I decided to let the police know my suspi-cions, officially, using Crime Stoppers. I could make the anonymous phone call, let them know what I was thinking, and let them deal with it. I was pretty sure that they would be interested in any information anyone could give at this time. And then tomorrow I could do the analysis I was being paid to do. I was part of the team now – even if no one was telling me anything. I had a job to do and a good reason to do it.

I sent a text to Trudy telling her that I'd be coming up for morning tea. I didn't mention why, of course, and I felt a little guilty misleading such a good friend. But I liked spending time with Trudy and that much was true. And also, if she asked, I'd tell her that I never wanted to give Joshua the opportunity to whinge to me again. That morning tea yesterday was so uncomfortable and awkward. Never again.

I would head up to the Biochemistry Department at around 11am and have a coffee there. In the meantime, I had work to do. I put on my lab coat and got started.

Boy did that feel good. Knowing what the day was going to hold and just getting in and ticking jobs off the list. I was focussed and slipped completely and easily into the work zone. I had missed this. Not the politics, not the funding applications, not the interesting people, but the work itself, I had missed this.

Once I had the instrument up and running again and had put on a new sample, I saved the output from the NMR that had run overnight onto a memory stick and went back to the desk to check it out. I had been told to use Eoin's desk – a big heavy wooden desk covered with piles of paper, scrap paper with scribbled notes, pens and pencils and erasers and rulers, and heavy reference books. I was pretty grateful that I could use the computer monitor to look at all the information – I wasn't sure I wanted to mess up the piles. They looked disorganised but maybe Eoin was the kind of guy that had an elaborate piling system. Not a filing system, he wasn't using files. Just a piling system – elaborate piles. And he hadn't been expecting anyone to use his desk while he was away on holidays. I had the feeling I could get in a lot of trouble if an important scrap of paper got lost.

The morning slipped away and the alarm came up on the computer telling me that it was time to head to morning tea. At the same time an email came in from Susannah, but I didn't make time to read it. I could do that after morning tea. Checking that everything was ticking along just fine with the instruments, I locked the office door and started the walk up the hill to the Biochemistry Department. The weather had broken, a lazy breeze from the south was blowing right through me and bringing spits of rain. A lovely Tasmanian summer's day. I hunched my shoulders and hoped that this front would pass soon, and was grateful that the Tassie weather had done its thing after the conference. While today felt like winter, it was perfectly normal summer weather on this island. It just didn't look good when tourists were treated to this. Of course, there were obviously some tourists fighting their way through the rain to see the various guidebook destinations, but at least they weren't tourists that I felt any sense of responsibility for.

By the time I had climbed the hill, I was sweating and puffing despite the cool rain. I truly needed to do more exercise. I was making plans to climb the hill twice a day while I was working at the uni. I could make these plans comfortably, knowing that I'd never carry them through.

Trudy got us a cup of tea and we sat at the table with the other staff. It was an interesting collection of people. They looked much more outdoorsy than the chemistry bunch. There was a lady, slim, tanned, dressed in a sleeveless tunic dress; a young guy with dreadlocks; an older man with a tweed jacket with leather patches on the elbows, and another who managed to wear a short-sleeved shirt and tie and still give the impression that he was ready to bush walk at a moment's notice. And there was Ken Jones with the wiry hair. The conversation around the table started with the weather, but fortunately (and probably quite understandably) Professor Conneally's death was still the talk of the town.

'I heard he started his career here,' I said, and the many and varied stories began – each person trying to out do the other.

There was the lecture where someone dressed as a gorilla swooped in and kidnapped a girl from the lecture theatre.

There was the lecture where Conneally burst into song to drive a point home 'Quite a good voice too' was the general opinion. There was some idea he was part of a choral group.

'He really was an excellent lecturer – his lectures were fun, full of stories and unexpected happenings, he kept the students engaged and managed to get his point across at the same time. Brilliant speaker. Such a loss.'

I agreed that his conference lecture was similarly brilliant and then asked, 'How did he treat his research students?'

'He only had a few students while he was here – nothing like the huge group he has now. Or had. It's so hard to think in past tense. Anyway, I think he was the chummy type of supervisor.'

'Yeah, group BBQs and curry nights, heading to the pub on a Friday night, first to show up, last to leave.'

'He did have that one student though, things went a bit badly then ...'

'That wasn't Conneally though, that was the student's fault.'

'Really? What happened there?' I had to push a bit then – people who are so eager to dish the dirt when someone is alive, are much less eager when they are gone. But finally someone reluctantly let it out.

'The story is that there was some cheating in a thesis. Or some such thing.'

I blurted out, 'a PhD thesis? How do you cheat in that?' I had never heard of anything like that before. And the group around the table weren't really sure of the full story.

'Plagiarism?'

'Nope, I think it was on the results from some of the tests – he was doing something with mice wasn't he?'

This was biochemistry, all the experiments were on either mice, or rats, or cell cultures derived from mice or rats. That was one reason

I avoided biochemistry. I much preferred to experiment with inanimate chemicals.

'It would have to be in the area of Motor Neurone Disease, right? That's where Prof Conneally works isn't it? Or worked ...'

'I can't quite remember, I think that some mice died that shouldn't have, something like that. Or they didn't report things from mice that lived and shouldn't have, or something.'

I took note of that. The older guy in the tweed jacket seemed to know what he was talking about. I was finding all this gossip incredibly interesting – it was making my brain move in new directions. But I wasn't getting the vibe I was expecting. There was no bitterness or anger about how people were used by the professor. The story that Trudy had told me before the conference wasn't coming up now. I wondered why.

I looked at Ken Jones to check his response but he looked completely at peace when discussing his old rival. There was no animosity there at all. I was a little confused. I kept digging.

'So did Prof Conneally leave because of the cheating?'

'There was a big fuss at the time, but I don't reckon that's why he left, but he did leave pretty soon after. He won an award or something that sent him over to the UK and the rest is history,' said dreadlocks.

'A meteoric rise to fame in just, what is it? Ten years?' tweed jacket asked.

'He really did make a name for himself. It's pretty devastating what has happened here – so much research that will now never happen,' said the lady in the tunic.

'Tragic really. You never know what a day will bring – one day you're doing fine, getting along like there's no problem at all, then the next, BAM! Heart attack and you're gone.' That was Ken Jones. I decided to introduce myself.

'Hi, I'm not sure we've met properly, I'm Alicia Conway – Trudy's friend. I'm working in chemistry right now' bit of a stretch but at least it made me look professional – better than unemployed.

'Ken Jones, pleased to meet you.'

'Were you here, Ken, when Prof Conneally was here?' I knew the answer but I had to start somewhere. Trudy was giving me funny looks but I ignored her, for now.

'Yes, we both started our careers at the same time and I'm still here. It's interesting how differently things can turn out. But then, life's a funny thing, hey.'

So he was open about how things had gone. How Conneally had risen to fame and he had just sat in the background. I tried to read between the lines – was there simmering resentment there? Or deeply hidden guilt? Had he done away with his rival and could now be content with where he was in life? I tried to frame a question that would give an incredibly insightful answer and would break the case wide open, but I couldn't think of anything at all to say. And while I was sitting there, composing questions, turning phrases in my mind, probably looking like the village idiot, the moment passed.

Jones turned to the rest of the table, 'We should organise a plaque or something to commemorate Conneally. Maybe something in the gardens? What do you all think?'

The rest of the staff discussed it happily. What kind of memorial would they have?

Where (most importantly) would the money come from to provide it? The discussion kept everyone around the table happily involved until they all left to go back to work.

I started to push back my chair but Trudy grabbed my arm.

'Alicia, what's going on? You were acting pretty strangely there – what are you trying to achieve?'

'Can we go somewhere private? Your office, perhaps?'

'What? My cubicle? In the office with the 11 other desks? Nah, we're better off here if we keep our voices down. Now, spill.'

Keeping my voice to a low murmur I told her that I suspected that Conneally's death was suspicious. And that I was trying to help with the investigation. Doing a bit of snooping to see what I could find out. I was pretty nervous, what if she had the same reaction as Jan and Nate? What if she told me just to leave it all to the police? Was I about to lose another friend? But no, Trudy was thrilled.

'Really? That's so exciting. I was there too – not at the dinner, but I was at the conference. I'll have a think about what I saw and I'll let you know if I think of anything suspicious. I'm not that observant, I know, but if I think of anything ...'

'Thanks Trudy, it's good to have someone onside. What do you think of Ken Jones as a suspect? Was he in Singapore last year?'

'Singapore? I think so. He had study leave. What I think of him as a suspect ... I'm not sure. He's not a very ... he's not a powerful man. He's not the type to take action about anything really. I can't see him taking any definitive action like murder.' Her voice dropped so low on the last word that I couldn't hear her at all, and had to read her lips.

'I just wonder. Twice he's talked about a 'heart attack' as the reason for death. He might be the type that's trying to point everyone's thoughts in the one direction – trying to deflect us from the actual cause of the murder. Sometimes the guys that have repressed everything get to the point where it all just boils out of them and they do something they later regret.'

'Does he look like he's regretting to you? And wouldn't you say that this, this, that all this had been planned?'

'I guess so, poison is not something you do in a fit of rage, is it? I'll keep thinking. And I'd better get back to work.'

'Yes, I had too. But I'll let you know if I think of anything.'

'Thanks Trudy, you're a real friend.'

'Ah Alicia, you bring excitement into my dull life.'

I walked back down the hill, my thoughts in overdrive. In the Biochemistry Department they work with life and death all the time. Was it possible to kill so many mice or rats that you find the step up to a human an easy step to take?

The chemistry building came into sight again and I remembered the email waiting for me and quickened my pace. The email turned out to be forwarded by Susannah from the coroner's office. They had (apparently) been given an anonymous tip about a student who was behaving suspiciously at the conference.

'Now, who could have given that tip?' I said to myself with a smile.

Conneally's ('the victim' was what was written in the email but I knew better) belongings had contained a note from that student and analysis of the note had shown traces of various chemicals. The email was to ask whether any of my analysis showed any connection to the list they had compiled from the note.

This was great! It would give me a starting place when analysing the NMR and MS results. The chemicals on the note were probably the reagents used to build the poison in the first place. The tip had gone somewhere and I was doing the right thing after all.

All thoughts of Ken Jones pushed out of my mind, I turned to the email, ready to get answers.

But I couldn't make it fit. The chemicals on the list weren't exotic reagents or starting materials. Most of them on the note were pretty innocuous – ammonia, well, that's everywhere. Acetate – just a normal lab day there. In fact, any molecule could have been made using any one of the chemicals at some point along the way. Maybe the note was written on paper taken out of a lab diary, that could explain everything.

To tell the truth, I was pretty unimpressed with whoever sent the email. The list was so unhelpful. Nothing could be absolutely linked to the sample I had. It wasn't evidence that would link Headphones Girl to the murder anywhere but in a gossip tabloid. Why were these people making noises about random chemicals. Everything is chemicals. They should know better.

I wondered what the note said. If it said 'You bastard, you let me down and I'm going to make your life hell from now on, as short as it will be' then sure, that's pretty incriminating, but they wouldn't need a chemical analysis to make anything stick from that, would they?

If it were an innocuous 'Dear Professor Conneally, I have decided that chemistry is totally boring and I wish to watch movies with my headphones on, whatever the situation, and become a professional critic instead' written on lab paper that she was never going to use again, then it wasn't particularly threatening.

Or how about, 'Dear Professor Conneally, I love your work and want to be your star pupil!! I will work for whatever you choose to give me and will make your professional dreams come true.' That one sounds especially incriminating to me – considering her behaviour at the conference. But the detectives wouldn't have that insight, would they? Not unless they asked me.

Regardless, whatever the note said, I couldn't find evidence that would pin Headphones Girl to the murder of Professor Conneally. It had to be someone else.

I turned back to the NMR results, matching them with the MS and the IR, playing with various ideas and options, piecing together a molecule that fit all the evidence. If there was a ring, attached to a carbonyl here ... that could work. There was still more analysis to go, the NMR was working flat out trying to find through-bond and through-space connections between atoms. But even without the final pieces of the puzzle I was going to have a good go at solving it. By the end of the day I had a few ideas – molecules A and B (imaginative names, I know). They looked right in terms of interpretation of the data but I'd never seen these kinds of molecules before. I had no idea how they'd work as a poison. It wasn't obvious at all. Maybe Susannah would have some idea. I looked at my watch, it was just after five. It's amazing how time goes when you're not thinking about it. That state of flow – how excellent it was. But was Susannah still in her office? Could I catch her before she went home? I sent my work to the printer and ran up the three flights of stairs to her office.

Running up the stairs wasn't such a great idea. I could see that Susannah's door was open so I took a moment to stop puffing and panting and to allow my heart to slow down, before I knocked on the door.

Susannah was chatting to Dan about his research but she waved me in and had a brief flick through the printed spectra while I explained my thoughts so far, keeping things as general as I could so that I wasn't spilling confidential information.

'I think I've got a fairly good handle on what the compound is,' I said as I handed her the data and my crudely drawn structures, 'I've got a couple of structures that would work well with the different spectra. But it doesn't match anything in the Mass Spec library and I'm pretty sure that the compounds found on that note don't work as reagents for the synthesis.'

Susannah agreed.

'Yes, you're right about the structures – I think it's more likely to be structure A than B though – those peaks are really downfield too far to be those methyls on B and the IR shows a nice carbonyl that works with structure A as well.'

'Do you think so? I was going with structure B. I'll have another look.'

'But you're right,' she went on, 'we still have no real answers. It really is a sad business isn't it? I should be cutting Joshua some slack I guess, it's not surprising that he's a bit upset. He used to study with Prof Conneally.'

'Did he? For Honours?'

'No, no. For a PhD.'

Dan was surprised and I was too. Though come to think of it, Trudy had pointed out a Joshua in that photo Professor Conneally had put in his talk. Was that the same Joshua? I remembered a photo of a clean-cut young lad in a white-collared shirt, bright smile on his face – nothing like the angry, messy, unreliable lab-tech that we knew and loved.

'Yes, he did years of post-graduate study. Back when Prof Conneally was a lowly lecturer here up at biochemistry.'

Dan was impressed. 'Wow, I didn't know that. Hang on, what jobs are there then? If Josh did all this like me and he's just a lab tech, what can I expect to get? I don't want to be stuck washing dishes for the rest of my life.'

Susannah put on her career adviser hat, and tried to calm Dan down by explaining how important it was to work in other universities after your PhD, and how it was looked on with favour by Australian universities if you could do a postdoctoral fellowship overseas, how it was important to get published in 'level A' journals and so on, but her words receded into the background for me.

Dan's question really was a good question. Why was Joshua washing up in a lab when he had done so much study? I needed to look into that. He should be at least working in industry somewhere, or doing research at a university. What had gone wrong? The big question was: had he graduated? Was he Dr Joshua? Did he actually (after all those years of post-graduate study) end up with a PhD?

Suddenly something clicked in my head. Everything fell into place. It all came together.

I interrupted, quite rudely, 'Susannah, what is Joshua's last name?'

She looked at me in surprise, 'Hume, Joshua Hume. Why do you want to know?'

'Thanks,' I said, and raced out the door.

I was about to run back up the hill to Biochemistry but I felt my aching legs and thought the better of it. I rang Trudy instead.

'Trudy, I need your help.'

'My help? Is everything ok?' I could hear panic in her voice and I felt so guilty. I could have phrased my request a bit less urgently, if I'd been feeling a little less urgent about it. Oops.

'Yes, yes, I'm fine. I just need to get some information from the biochemistry records. Are you still at work?'

'Oh I'm sorry Alicia, I leave at 3pm most days to pick up the kids from school, and I'm actually making dinner now. Could it possibly wait until tomorrow? Or I could try to contact someone else for you.' Emergency over, Trudy prioritised her life correctly, family was put first as it should be.

Could it wait? I nearly tore out my hair with frustration, the curiosity was getting overwhelming and I wondered whether I would be able to sleep at all, but it probably could wait. I didn't want anyone else involved, and I didn't want to pull Trudy away from her family for a wild goose chase. After all, I wasn't completely sure.

'If I came up tomorrow first thing, would I be in the way? You're not teaching or anything?'

'No, yes, come on over. I'll meet you in the foyer.'

'Thanks so much Trudy, it will be so helpful!'

'What do you need our records for anyway?'

'Ah, look it's a bit complicated. I'll tell you tomorrow.'

So that was that. Everything was put off until the next day and I needed to sit on my thoughts and wait. I wasn't going to do anything without firm evidence this time. I needed to be absolutely sure. It was time to go home and try to relax.

I stepped through the cottage door and placed the keys carefully on the hall table. Turning my stereo on, I moved to the kitchen to try to find inspiration for food for myself.

'Why do we have to eat all the time?' I asked out loud as I stared into the fridge hoping for a delicious and easy idea to spontaneously form in my brain or to spontaneously form in my fridge so I could just take it out and eat it. Where were the sci-fi dinner pills when you needed them? No matter how long I stared, I couldn't work out what I wanted. In the end I gave up on the healthy option and went for fish and chips from the corner store. The sky was clear and blue with wispy white clouds sitting on the horizon and the air was beautifully balmy. I could go for a nice long walk along the beach at the same time as picking up my dinner and perhaps get the swirling thoughts in my head into order. Maybe even exhaust myself enough so that I would sleep.

The weather had improved so much from this morning's cool breeze and showers of rain and it looked like all the local inhabitants had also decided to go for an evening walk. I met and greeted several of my mother's old friends as I wandered along the beach barefooted in the rippling waves. I greeted quite a few people I didn't know as well. That was the way down here – everyone you passed gave you a friendly 'Hi' or 'Good evening' or 'Lovely night, isn't it?'

It was a really delightful aspect of a small town that you had this community around at all times. I could see that it might get a bit overwhelming if anonymity is what you were craving but I enjoyed the off-the-cuff conversations and the greetings as I walked along the street (or beach as it may be). It was a friendly way to live.

Then the community became a whole lot less comforting because I saw Jan and Nate in the distance. What to do? I didn't really want to talk with Nate. Not yet. Not without evidence. What would I say? What on earth could we talk about that didn't involve the Conneally case, that didn't encroach on awkward territory? A quick 'Hi' and moving on would not be enough.

Had they seen me?

As quickly as I could (trying not to draw attention to myself) I walked back up to the footpath and tried to hide behind the trees and cars lining the beach. If I could just make it to the take-away on the corner … they would never go in there. I could hide in there. I would be safe.

Just two more cars … one more … I was so nearly there – but no, Jan was waving. Could I pretend I didn't see her? Not really. I pasted a smile on my face and headed back to the beach again to say hello. Crazy isn't it? In my head, when I'm not around them, I'm so angry that they have ignored me and not let me in on their secret, but I don't have the guts to tell them so. I can't be the one to break up the relationship. Passive-aggressive me. Disaster.

'How is the work going?' Jan wanted to know. I could keep that safe, I guess, if they didn't ask pointed questions about what I was working on.

'Really good. I'm really enjoying it, feeling like I'm getting somewhere.' Nice vague answer. And Nate took the conversation to an easy place.

'Do you think they'll keep you on after this?'

I shrugged.

'It's very unlikely. They just can't do it. If they want to employ someone permanently there needs to be this whole big process. The uni is always bragging about how its workforce are so internationally first-class and all. They can't just employ whoever they like.'

'But you are first-class.'

'Aww Jan, you're so supportive, but the difficulty is persuading the Human Resources Department and the Provost.'

'What's a Provost?'

'He's the guy that holds the purse strings for the university and makes the overall funding and staffing decisions.'

'Do you know who he is? Could you go and talk with him?' Nate was really trying to solve my problem for me.

'It just doesn't work that way. I'm going to have to wait and see if someone has research funding and can take me on, or wait for a job to come up. I don't really like my chances though, I think I'll have to head back to the mainland eventually.'

'Back to the mainland? You don't want to do that. Surely there's something available here, surely something will come up.'

'The problem is that I'm trained to work at a university, to do research, and here in Hobart there's only the one small Chemistry Department. If I want to work here, I'm waiting to fill a dead man's shoes and the staff here are young – not likely to die anytime soon.'

'I have an idea, you're a chemist – you could make some poison and kill one of the lecturers off. Shouldn't be too hard.' Jan said with a smile.

'That's a bit close for comfort.' I said, laughing.

And Nate agreed, 'Too soon Jan, too soon.'

Jan gasped. 'Oh the guy who died, oh Alicia, I'm so sorry. I wasn't thinking.'

I reassured her that I was fine, and tried to figure out whether it was safe to talk about this yet. It felt a bit like an opening to ask Nate if they had found out what or who had killed him. But then, it was all a bit awkward really. Nate seemed to think so too and tried to change the subject back.

'So you think you're going to have to move away again? Is there a place you'd prefer to go?'

We had a bit more desultory conversation then about the various places I'd worked, and where I'd prefer to live. But while we were standing on the beach in the long Tasmanian twilight, it was difficult to imagine anywhere I'd rather be. There wasn't anywhere else I'd rather be, to be frank. I realised I had got used to it here – the pace of life, the beauty of nature all around, the quiet, the community. Where would I go? And how would I live if I stayed?

I didn't have to answer those questions right away though, I had (thanks to Mum's money management skills) time to make up my mind. And maybe I could keep getting little jobs at the uni for a while and stretch things out a bit. I would have to see how it all went.

It was all a bit awkward – they were asking questions I didn't have answers for, and I had questions front and centre in my brain that I didn't want to ask them right now. I was glad when they decided to move on and I could go and buy my fish and chips.

I thought about the drawbacks to working at a university, I wondered if Nate struggled with pressure and politics, surely he did. I couldn't imagine the Police Department being free from those kinds of pressures. Maybe he just let it wash off his back. Did Jan have to deal with politics too, working at the café? Was owning your own business the way to go? Setting your own hours? But I had never wanted to do that – never wanted the responsibility of being the boss. I just wanted to be able to do my work well and enjoy it. Would I ever get that opportunity again?

'That was moderately uncomfortable,' said Nate to Jan as they walked away.

'What? Oh, I didn't think. Alicia's been so happy to come and talk with me at the café.'

'I don't think she's all that happy to talk with me yet.' Jan and Nate continued to walk along the beach, dodging sandcastles and bits of driftwood.

'Is that why you grabbed my arm and tried to push me down to the water?'

'Yes, that would be it. But you'd already started waving.'

'Ah well, it didn't go too badly did it?' Jan skirted a trench dug in the sand.

'I guess not. She wasn't eager to stay but at least she didn't storm off like last time.'

'You can't tell her anything you're working on yet, can you?'

'Nope. Not a thing. But at least she didn't ask. I wonder why she didn't ask?' Nate stopped to pick up a stick and throw it into the waves.

'Well, maybe she's so happy to have this work at the uni that it's distracted her from trying to find invisible murderers.'

'I'll be able to tell her everything soon, I'm sure.'

'Well, until then I'll do my best to keep you two apart.'

'Great. I wish we'd had this conversation before you did your waving thing.'

'Can't have everything Nate.'

I had decided to park a little closer to the biochemistry building so that I wouldn't have to walk so far up the hill. The parking was easy if you were prepared to park a few streets away from the uni and walk for a bit, but if you wanted to be close, you had to get there early. So I'd made a quick start to the day. Even if I had to sit for a while waiting for

Trudy to make it in to work, (a highly likely occurrence) it would be ok.

It was another beautiful morning. White fluffy clouds and a blue sky. The summer light in Tasmania was awesome, the days so long. Getting up early wasn't too hard when the sky started to lighten at four am and the sun rose at five. The roads were still quiet – just a few cars making their way in to the city to start work.

It was a morning so peaceful and so full of promise. I couldn't help it, I felt light hearted and ready for anything. But as I became aware of how great I felt, guilt rose in my mind like a cloud. How could I feel this light-hearted, knowing that somewhere Mrs Conneally was still grieving, not to mention the rest of the Professor's relatives, knowing that Lisa's future was uncertain unless she could find another supervisor, and most of all thinking that somewhere in this city was a person who was able to deliberately kill another human being and cause so much pain to so many people? But somehow, as I drove through the still of the morning, all of that seemed like something I had read in a novel last night, and the light, the blue of the sky and the olive green of the gum trees, the clear air and the peace seemed to be the real world.

And maybe this was the real world. Maybe one day all of the hurt and pain, the bitterness and anger, would pass away and the peace and joy held in this beautiful summer morning would be all that remained. I often wondered about that. Wondered what the new heaven and the new earth would be like once all this damaged world was gone.

Maybe the little moments of joy in the car, the summer light and the colours, were put there, right in the middle of such pain and anger, as a reminder that there is more, even in this life, than the pain and hate that can seem all consuming.

I remembered having moments like this when my mum was ill. Little specks of light in the midst of great darkness, and how they helped me through. I prayed that Mrs Conneally was experiencing the same moments of lightness even now and that she knew how to take advantage of them.

As I crested the hill and started the downward run to the university I could not help but rejoice in the sight. Hobart was such a beautiful city. The river glistened in the morning light and even this early there were a few yachts out with their spinnakers up. The lovely old houses of Battery Point clustered under the spire of the Anglican church never ceased to delight me. That inner-city suburb of Hobart was like an old English village – walking around there always brought Midsomer Murders to mind. And there was the bridge spanning the river, not as iconic as the Sydney Harbour Bridge, but still an icon to anyone who loved this tiny city.

I found a park on the hill near the biochemistry building (it was worth the early start) and took my mind away from these lovely thoughts and back to the question at hand. It was Dan's question that echoed in my head. Why did Joshua have a lab tech job when he had done so much study? That was the key to the whole puzzle. The missing piece. But I knew I would have to find some proof, some evidence.

And I felt so bad for poor Joshua. If my hunch was correct, his life must have been so awful, and I couldn't imagine what would be going through his brain right now. Even if it was just that he had never finished his PhD. Imagine putting in all that effort but never actually getting the piece of paper, never doing the walk at the graduation with the floppy hat. But I was scared that there was much more of a connection between Joshua and the dead professor.

Trudy found me sitting out on the front steps of the biochemistry building, wishing I had stopped for coffee on the way in.

'Morning! How are we this morning? What exactly do you want to look at here?' she asked.

'I need to see files, any files, from that PhD thesis that was canned for cheating. I'm pretty sure you'll find that it belongs to one Joshua Hume.'

'Joshua?! The guy who works for Susannah? That Joshua?'

'One and the same. Do you have any idea where we'd find his old lab books or anything at all about it?'

'Now what year was that? Oh dear, I have no idea but I know where any records will be. Come and see the lovely windowless back closet where we keep all of the paperwork that we just can't throw away. You can look through the boxes, I'll try the computer archives and see if there's anything left on the server. Knowing the name will be helpful but you never know how people will save their stuff. He might have a folder in his own name but you know, because we want the files, you can bet they will be stored under something random.'

Trudy led me to the storage space behind the main lecture theatre, unlocked the door, and let me in. I looked around, and gathered my courage for the job ahead. In the dark and dreary space lit by a single hanging bulb was a row of compactors full of badly labelled boxes, books, and even loose papers. Over on one side was a small bench space that I thought I might be able to use as I sorted through the flotsam and jetsam of years of university research. All of the teaching props were also squeezed in here: preserved and mounted samples of body parts, organs, and diseased pieces of flesh rubbed shoulders with human anatomy statues, and to add to the mess, rolled up posters from previous conference sessions were stacked against one wall, getting accidentally creased and squashed by even more boxes filled with old exam papers. It was not the most spacious place and a bit spooky to be honest, and I was grateful that I wasn't claustrophobic. Who knew how much time it would take to find what I wanted?

Trudy propped the door open and I stole a chair from the lecture theatre and set up at the bench. I'd try to find boxes labeled with dates from ten years ago and see what I could find. If that didn't work, I would have to start on the mysterious unlabelled boxes. I hoped it wouldn't come to that.

'I'll leave you to it – I'll come and dig you out at around lunch time if I don't see you before. I'll go look in the electronic records and see what I can find.'

'Hopefully the records aren't password protected – I don't want to bring Nate in on this until I'm absolutely sure.'

'We'll do what we have to do – you know I'll have to leave at 3pm to take boys to soccer practice.'

'Don't spend too much time on this Trudy. I have all the time in the world but you are one of the busiest people I know.'

'Of course I'm going to spend time on this. This is the most exciting thing that's happened to me in years. Catching a killer. How brilliant is this?'

Trudy raced off to her office and I dug into the mountain of work. I wouldn't have thought that I'd ever want to spend time in a little cupboard like this, sorting through someone else's paperwork, but it's amazing what you'll do when you think there's a reason to do it. I wasn't put off by the mess much at all, I was almost as excited as Trudy.

Now, back ten years and look under C. Or maybe J. Or H. Hmmm.

A couple of hours later I was still hard at it. I held one box up against the bench with my knee and tried to sort through it with one hand while keeping it steady with the other. My neck and shoulders hurt from lugging the boxes around. My back hurt from getting into all sorts of strange positions trying to find the right boxes. My eyes hurt from trying to read the lab diary notes by the meagre rays fighting through the dust coated on the lonely light bulb. Still the tiny bench top was piled with books and notes that might be meaningful and I'd searched my way through almost every box in the room. There was no way that I'd be able to put it all together in this tiny space though, I needed room to breathe and spread out.

I pulled up the last few pages in the box. I had this to say for Joshua, he definitely worked hard. I had so many lab books with his name on them, and yep, here were some more notes, they looked like journal article drafts or thesis drafts – nicely typed up and covered with the red and green pen of supervisor feedback. I put them in the pile with the other drafts, put the box back on the floor and stretched my aching back.

Trudy popped her head in the door.

'How are you going?'

'I'm getting there I think. This looks to be most, if not all, of his stuff. I can't look at it properly here though. Do you think it would be alright if I took it home?'

'I'm sure it would be fine. No one has looked at these for over ten years. They won't miss them if you don't tell them.'

'Well, I won't be here to tell them. So it's up to you.'

'Ha. That's a good point. Anyway, I have something to show you too. It looks like various drafts of a thesis. If you compare it with the lab diaries you might be able to get to the bottom of it all. I've put all I could find on a memory stick for you, it's pretty jumbled I'm afraid.'

'No worries. I'll take these and that and perhaps go home where I can be more comfortable. I'll bring it all back, don't worry.' I put the USB key into my pocket. Then I moved the remaining papers in one half-emptied box into another that was also now half-empty and sorted my piles of papers into the empty box. The mess on the bench I managed to cram into two boxes and Trudy helped me to tidy away all the other boxes of notes and lab diaries.

'It's not really well catalogued anymore, if it ever was. But it will have to do. You can blame me if it ever causes problems.'

'Want a hand getting that to the car?'

The two of us made short work of packing the paperwork into my car and Trudy wished me good luck as she waved goodbye.

'Let me know how you get on. It's actually pretty exciting being part of the team ...'

'Sure, I will. I think I have a rather less than exciting afternoon and evening coming up but I'm pretty sure I'm on the right track now. Getting more sure all the time.'

I was also absolutely sure that there was no way I could get a coherent story out of the pile of books and papers in the boot of my car without a large shot of caffeine. I wouldn't stay at The Lemon Tree though, I needed to keep going now, the information in those papers was calling to me and I was pretty sure the answer I needed was there. I was a miner, searching for information, just like so many other times in my research career, but this time there was more urgency – someone's life hung on this, justice hung on getting the information right, and I knew that if the killer was caught, Mrs Conneally would have the chance to move on with her life – she wouldn't be stuck forever asking 'why?'.

I pulled up at my little cottage and lugged the boxes into the house. I made myself a quick sandwich to have with the coffee and prepared for an afternoon of hard work. I cleared all the surfaces in the lounge room, grabbed a notebook and my laptop, and sorted through the boxes for the first laboratory diary and a draft of the thesis. I was determined to find out what had happened during Joshua's PhD. I was sure that this was the key to the whole mystery.

Everything gets written in the lab diaries. They are the record of what happens daily in research, the place where everything is laid out – the good, the bad, and the ugly. And when you take what you've done in three years of PhD research and compile it to make a PhD thesis, you generally leave out the ugly, and sometimes you leave out the bad. But sometimes the bad things are part of the whole story and need to be included. If they are left out, then people get the wrong impression, especially when you are talking about drug discovery.

So that was what I was looking for. I wanted to find something that was in the lab diaries, but was not in the thesis drafts. Something that had been left out that should have been kept in.

I needed an overview of the project, so I started with the abstract. It looked like Joshua was working on a pretty important topic. Here it was: 'Sometimes called Motor Neurone disease, or Lou Gehrig's disease, Amyotrophic Lateral Sclerosis (ALS) attacks the nervous system and hinders the ability of the brain to control the muscles.' Nasty stuff! I read through Joshua's description of the disease progress. What a horrible way to die. You can't move, you can't eat, and eventually you can't even breathe. Good on Joshua and Professor Conneally for working on this one. A truly noble cause.

The next part of the abstract explained the work they were doing to fix the problem.

They were looking into some novel prospective drugs – chemicals that would stimulate the nervous system and keep the patients alive and active for longer. And in Joshua's case, the patients were mice.

Now that I had some idea of the overview of the project I went back over the lab books, looking for chemical names and mouse records. As I went through the pages I could see the results of the testing, all nicely labelled with the various drug codes.

It was really neat way of testing too. The feet of the mice were dipped in paint and then they were made to walk along a paper path. I could see that when the mice were sick, their feet dragged, the footprints overlapped. I could imagine the poor little mice trying to pull themselves along the paper and not being able to move properly. It was a pathetic image.

There was the path for the control mice, and then as the diaries went on there were different traces of mice being treated with different drugs. To be honest, there wasn't a lot of change in the footprints for quite a long time. They'd start out firm and well defined but in no time at all they would deteriorate and the mice would die.

But then, in the third lab book a new chemical appeared. When the mice were given this chemical, this potential drug the footsteps stayed firmer for much longer, the prints were much better defined. The little mice were veritably marching along the page. The treatment gave the little mice a much longer life span, and a few weeks for mice could translate into years, or decades for humans.

I cross-checked between lab diary records and the drafts of the thesis and papers that Trudy had given me on the memory stick. It looked like great news. In fact, I was getting excited. The sick mice were responding so well. This drug could be a real success story. I wondered if it could even be useful to help treat more diseases than just ALS. Maybe multiple sclerosis, maybe Parkinsons ...

But then reality came crashing back in, there was Joshua washing dishes in the lab. If this drug was the big success story that it looked, then he would be sailing on a yacht in the Caribbean. Or at least working for a large pharmaceutical company in a big city somewhere. Something must have gone wrong. I wondered what it was.

I kept working through the lab diaries, following the progress of the mice that were being treated with the new wonder drug and cross-checking diary charts with the PhD thesis drafts. I found the answer in the fourth lab book. Suddenly pages were scored with scrawls of 'Why???' and 'WTF???' and 'Argh!!'. The mice were dying. Not the sick mice, they were still doing fine, but Joshua had given some of the potential drug to healthy mice as a control and the healthy mice were dying.

I followed through the pages and found some sentences that interested me greatly.

'Healthy mice that receive a dose have symptoms that look like a heart attack. PM on mice shows no atherosclerosis. Nervous system was over stimulated leading to death.'

The symptoms of the healthy mice were exactly the same as those of Professor Conneally. That looked like pretty serious evidence against Joshua. This was a strong indication of his involvement.

There had to be a page somewhere that told me what this chemical was. Something more than UL0710 – the code he had given it.

Biochemists drive me mad. Don't they care what the actual structure looks like? Surely it's the way the chemical is made that does the job. I looked through books and pages and article drafts. Finally I found a table with all the structures of the different drugs he was using in his experiments.

There it was. UL0710. Looking just like one of the structures I had sketched from my analysis. When things calmed down again and I was in a position to gloat I would have to tell Susannah that the structure was more like my structure B than my structure A. I got it right.

But right now this was more evidence. Joshua was definitely involved. And why? I was pretty sure I knew. The gossip at the bio-chemistry building had made it fairly obvious.

Now I turned to the thesis for evidence. If the healthy mice were dying, it should have been recorded for publication somewhere. You can't leave out information like that.

There had been nothing about possible side-effects (death is a pretty serious side-effect too) in the abstract so I looked elsewhere. I searched electronically, I searched the piles of papers, the printed sheets of thesis drafts, the early drafts of journal articles, there was no mention of the deaths of healthy mice anywhere in any of it. The lounge room started to look like a mountain in the alps, like it had snowed paper – there were paper drifts on the floor, on every chair, on every surface. But apart from in the lab diaries themselves there was no trace of the information that the healthy mice had died. Nothing.

Obviously this was it. This is the big issue that caused the end of Joshua's career. This was the disaster. This was the cheating in the PhD thesis.

It didn't have to be a disaster, though. It could have been dealt with correctly and Joshua would still have had a worthy PhD thesis. I wondered just what went wrong in the end. Did Joshua decide not to include this very important problem with his new drug lead, thinking it would mean the thesis could not be published, and he would not gain his doctorate? Did Conneally tell him that it would be ok, that others would find the problem later and that he could go ahead without it? And how was it found out? And how was Joshua told that his career was over?

I was sure that this time I had found the person responsible for the murder of Professor Conneally. Joshua had to be the one to have poisoned the professor. And with his wonder drug too.

But how? He hadn't been anywhere near the restaurant. I hadn't seen him there at all that night – Misaki, Robbie and I had carefully examined all of the delegates in our time-wasting before our meal was served. We were closely watching everyone at the table. Joshua was not there.

But he'd done it somehow. I knew he was involved. And one way to find out how, was to ask.

I had driven to the university, found a place to park the car, and tried to figure out how I would begin the conversation with Joshua. How did one start to accuse someone of murder? 'Joshua, I think it's time you confessed' what authority did I have to say that? Or 'Would you like to tell me the story of how you murdered Conneally?' Not really smooth. I prayed that I'd find the words once I got there. And that Susannah would be happy to work with me. So much could go wrong. My stomach tightened and my mouth felt dry. How would he respond?

I knocked on Susannah's office door.

'Hi Susannah, I need to interrupt whatever you're doing. I'm sorry but this is really important.'

Susannah looked up from her computer, 'Of course. I'm intrigued. What do you need?'

'I need two things – I need a private conversation with Joshua, maybe you could bring him here? And I need someone, maybe Dan, to look in Joshua's office and lab and in the waste for vials or containers or anything labelled UL0710 or anything with the label recently ripped off, or anything with a structure matching this one.'

Susannah looked at the structure I showed her and her eyes widened.

'Joshua?' it didn't take much for her to put two and two together. I had always known this woman was brilliant, but I was impressed.

'I'm almost completely sure.'

'Have you told the police?'

'I'm only almost completely sure. That's why I'm here.'

'Ok, I'll put Dan and Liv onto the searching and I'll bring Joshua here. But I'm not leaving. This could get dangerous.'

Susannah left the office and I sat and waited, once again running through my head the possible openers for the difficult conversation ahead.

'What's going on? What do you need to talk to me about?' I heard the defensive grumble coming up the hallway.

'Actually Joshua, it's me that wants to talk to you,' I said, 'have a seat.'

He sat down, glancing at the door where Susannah stood, trying to look casual. I gathered my thoughts and started to talk. I told

Joshua all that I had found out about his past. That he was a student under Prof Conneally, and a good and clever one at that, and that they discovered something very exciting. A possible treatment for motor neurone disease.

Joshua stared at me as I spoke. His jaw dropped open and he kept shaking his head like he couldn't believe what he was hearing. And then he spoke, suspicious and cautious, 'Yeah, you're right. It was a breakthrough.'

'But something went wrong, didn't it? I've looked at your books, your lab diaries. Some of the mice were dying.'

'How did you find that out? I thought it all would have been thrown out years ago! Why are you telling me all this?'

'Is it true though? Can you tell me about it?'

There was a long silence, and I was scared that he'd get up and leave the room. I looked up at Susannah and she stood a little straighter, blocking the doorway. Then Joshua decided to speak.

'I guess so. Yeah, some mice were dying. The healthy ones. The controls. The sick mice – the transgenic mice – they were great on the drug. Did you see the footprint trace? It took them so much longer to get sick, and they lasted a whole month longer than we thought they would.'

'Only a month, then they died?' said Susannah shrugging her shoulders, 'Didn't you want them to get better?'

Joshua looked at Susannah with eyes full of contempt, 'They don't get better. This is neuron damage, not a grazed knee. All we're trying to do is give a better quality of life, a longer life. A month with a mouse is equivalent to years, maybe even decades of human life. Don't you know anything?' His fists clenched and unclenched on his knees and I watched and worried. This was getting scary. What was I going to do if he got violent?

'So, you got excellent results for the sick mice then ...' would the distraction calm him down?

'It was unreal, really excellent. Longer life, later onset, just amazing.' Joshua leant towards me, his hands waving as he explained the medical breakthrough. Susannah relaxed and leant against the door frame. I realised that I had never seen Joshua this animated, that talking about his research was tapping into a part of him that had been pushed down and hidden all this time. What I had thought was his normal way of being was probably a super depressed state. All these years, pushing down all the desires of his heart. Hope deferred makes the heart sick. This guy had been sick for a decade.

I didn't want to lose the happy Joshua again by bringing back his depression, but unfortunately it had to be done. I had to get to the bottom of it all. Whether he got violent or not.

'The dead mice?' I prompted and Joshua retreated back into his shell.

'Yeah, the dead mice. Like I said, the sick mice improved massively, but when we gave the drug to the healthy mice they died.'

'Why do you think they died?' I probed.

'It was like, I dunno, maybe the drug stimulated the heart too much and the healthy system couldn't cope. It always looked like a heart attack but we would check and there were no signs of heart disease so we figured it was a nervous system thing.'

'But you didn't write about that in your thesis?'

I kept my tone gentle, understanding, I wanted to get to the emotional reasons why Joshua had felt that murder was the only option. I wanted to help him to see what he had done.

'Conneally said not to. No-one believes me, but it's true. He said it wasn't part of the story. He said that the main idea in my thesis was that the sick mice got healthy. That the issue with the controls would only be important later, when the drug was being patented or improved, or whatever – somewhere in a trial before it was being sold to the public. So no, I didn't write that bit up.'

'And you went ahead and submitted the thesis for examination.'

'Yeah, I submitted.'

Joshua became silent again.

'So?' I prompted after what felt like an age, 'What happened?'

'What do you expect? An examiner's report came back asking about controls. He said that the thesis wasn't complete without the bit about the healthy mice. He asked whether we had done any experiments with healthy mice at all. So of course we said yes, and we gave the results, and then it all hit the fan. I was accused of hiding the negatives, and it all went higher up and Conneally just dropped the lot on me – didn't take any of the blame himself. Told them I'd hidden it all from him, that I'd fudged the figures.'

'And you know this because ...'

'It's obvious isn't it?' his fists clenched and he kicked the desk in front of him, 'What else would have happened? They threw me out, they threw all my research in the bin, kicked me out for malpractice or whatever. I was done.'

'And you blamed the professor.' Boy I was working hard at keeping my tone low. I wanted to defuse the tension here and he was getting pretty worked up. Not that I should have expected anything else – I was really poking at a sore spot. I wondered where this would all end up. I glanced at Susannah. She wasn't leaning against the door frame anymore. She was poised ready to jump into action, to come to my rescue if needed. But we had to keep going now.

'It was his fault. All of my years of study and research down the drain and nothing to show for it. No three letters after my name – no Joshua Hume PhD, no Dr Joshua. No respect for what I'd done. He took it all from me. Such a waste of my time. A waste of years of my life. Did he suffer? Not at all. Next thing I know he's off to Cambridge. Climbing the ladder at the speed of light. And I'm here, washing dishes. Couldn't get any other jobs. Who would employ someone who had wasted literally years of their life doing work that led nowhere, with no references, no nothing?'

'You must have thought that life was playing into your hands to bring Conneally back here ...'

Joshua slumped back in his chair and stared at the floor. 'All the stars aligned. Everything came together. If you're wondering how I still had some of that drug, I took it when I left the uni. Even then I was thinking of how I could get my own back. Such a long wait, but it finally happened. I got Sally to get work at the conference dinner. You know, Hobart's a small place and it's all about who you know. I knew people and Sally knew people.'

Who was Sally?I looked at Susannah and she shrugged. I didn't want to stop the flow of words here, but I wondered what this Sally was like. I mean, Joshua looked like the brains of the operation but there was another person out there who was willing to commit murder. And if she knew that we'd found Joshua, what was going to happen to us? How could we find her? We had no idea who she was but she could easily find us if she wanted to. I wondered if we were in danger, I think the same thought had occurred to Susannah too – she was glancing back over her shoulder occasionally, and rubbing her hands. We were both pretty uncomfortable with what was coming out. But Joshua didn't really notice, he just kept talking.

'It was easy. Sally didn't know what I was planning of course. She had no idea of what the drug could do. And neither did I, really, I mean I'd only given it to mice. Who knew if it would work on a human? It was the great human trial, n=1.'

'And it worked. And he died.'

'And he died, yes. That was what I was hoping for, a successful trial.' Joshua wiped his face with his hands. 'He's dead and it's over. Nothing will bring him back. He is actually dead. I played this out so many times in my head, but now it's happened. Dead. And so many people affected by this, not just him, but his family, his students, his colleagues, his friends, they are all changed by this. I hadn't thought ...'

'How do you feel?'

Joshua shifted in his seat, 'I don't know why I am telling you this, but I feel shit. It's not what I thought, I thought I'd feel, you know, like, victorious, happy, something. But I just feel guilty, just massive guilt. I can't face Sally, how could I make her kill someone? How could I do that to anyone? I can't face anyone. I can't stop thinking about it.'

I wondered whether Sally was really that innocent. Did she really not know what was going to happen? I mean, you don't just poison someone for kicks. How would I find her? What kind of person was she?

At least Joshua looked like he was calm again. In fact, he looked like someone who had gone through counselling – like telling someone all about it was what he'd been dying to do for years. Maybe I should be looking for a new career.

'Josh, are you ready to turn yourself in?'

'Do you think,' Josh looked up at me, through unshed tears, 'do you think, if I do that, I'll get peace? I thought his death would end the thoughts in my head but it's just made them ten times worse.'

'I don't know,' I said, 'but I reckon it's the beginning to the path of peace. It's a long path, but turning yourself in will be a good start.'

Joshua hung his head as his thoughts turned inwards. I wasn't sure what to do next but I could see that Joshua was earnest about wanting it all to be over. His bitterness had strangled all the life out of him for the last ten years. I could only feel sorry for him.

I looked at Susannah standing in the door and staring at Joshua. She looked a bit wild around the eyes. It would be stressful to realise you were the boss of a person who was willing to murder if they didn't get their own way. But Susannah hadn't been in any danger really. Joshua had been totally taken up with Conneally for the past decade. It was amazing that he had got any work done at all.

Neither Susannah nor myself had any idea what to do next. But I knew someone who knew. I pulled the phone out of my pocket to finally call Nate.

But before I could make the call, I was interrupted by the sound of slamming doors and racing footsteps.

The office door burst open and Nate charged in followed by a couple of police officers in uniform.

'Police! Stay right there!' he shouted at Joshua, 'Don't try anything!'

Joshua looked up with a weary 'Huh?'

'Joshua Hume, I am arresting you for the murder of Professor James Conneally. You do not have to say anything but anything you do say will be taken in evidence.'

Joshua nodded calmly.

'Oh good,' he said with obvious relief, 'thanks.'

That stopped Nate in his tracks. 'Thanks? What?'

'You've saved him a lot of trouble,' I responded with a laugh, 'he was just trying to figure out how to turn himself in. He's never been in this situation before and he didn't know where to start.'

Joshua went quietly with the police officers, only stopping to ask me to go and see Sally and pass on his apology to her. I promised to do my best.

Once Joshua was safely down the hallway and out of earshot I turned to Nate.

'Nate, who is Sally?'

'Alicia, what have you done?'

'Looks like there's a lot of explaining to be done all round,' said Susannah.

'Yes, but not here. I think you're going to have to come to the station with me too.'

I felt totally drained, I looked around me for my bag and phone and was gathering myself to follow Nate when Dan burst into the office waving some sample vials and yelling, 'Found it, found the poison!'

Nate looked from Dan to me with such incredulity that I sank back into my chair and giggled hysterically. It had been a long day.

The day didn't get any shorter. There's no way that you can discover a murderer and not incur a considerable amount of paperwork. Everyone who had been involved needed to go to the police station and make a statement. Susannah, Dan, Liv, Trudy and myself all had to give our little bit of evidence. And I had to go back to the mess in my lounge room and put aside all the important papers and hand them and all the boxes to Nate and his team. It was about midnight when I finally dropped into bed but Nate assured me that we could meet at The Lemon Tree the next day and I'd get all my questions answered.

We all met at The Lemon Tree – Nate, Jan, and myself, but also Trudy, Susannah, Dan and Liv. Everyone needed to hear what this was about. I gave my side of the story – missing out a few of the more embarrassing side tracks. I didn't want to look stupid, after all.

'So that was the thing that set me on the right track. The gossip from the Biochemistry Department, Joshua's incredibly bad attitude, and the knowledge that he had not completed a PhD, it all came together somehow in my head.'

'But surely, it's not that important – just for some letters after your name, surely it's not worth killing for.' Jan was still struggling to come to terms with the motive.

'It's a rarified environment. We all tell each other how important we are, and suddenly all you can see worth living for is the appellation 'Professor'. You begin to believe that these people are a higher life form. You have to believe that to make it worth working for. Joshua's ideas were only slightly more twisted than that.' Susannah responded to my statement with a frown. This was her world, her ambition. Maybe there was a purer motive for wanting to get ahead in academia, but after this adventure I was feeling a bit cynical.

I decided to change the subject, 'Nate, we need to hear about Sally. Who was she? What was all that about?'

'Yes, Nate, tell us the whole story – why did you end up rushing in like that? Give us all the gory details.' Susannah added.

'It's a bit of a long story ...'

'This is a coffee shop, Nate. We're all good for drink and food. Just spit it out ...'

This is the story Nate told:

'The thing is, Alicia, after you came to our house in such a state, I decided to look into this whole thing thoroughly. It's not that I thought you were right, as such, but you obviously would have needed some pretty strong information to change your mind and let you think that everything was ok. I didn't really know how to prove to you that there was nothing to worry about, but I was going to have a good try.'

'You know that there's no such thing as proving a negative?'

'Yes, I know, but you were really concerned and Jan here wanted to be able to calm you down. We were worried for you. So I looked into things a bit more carefully, just to make sure that there was absolutely no chance of foul play.'

Nate had pored over the post mortem. He had gone back to the restaurant and searched the place high and low. It was Nate who had found the little glass vial in the rubbish and had asked for it to be analysed as soon as possible. It was starting to look like there was evidence of foul play after all.

He continued his investigation by interviewing the restaurant staff.

The first on the list was the manager, Malcolm Edwards. Edwards was a small plump man, round body, round head, round glasses, overly aware of his own importance and not necessarily inclined to be too helpful to the police.

He had pointed out where the VIP table had been set up – right near the open fire. And, yes, the professor had been one of those with a planned and special seat.

'Who knew about the special table? Who knew which people were especially singled out?'

'Well, there was the events manager.'

Nate waited, his pen poised over his notebook.

'Kate, Kate Stevenson.'

Nate noted that down and waved for the manager to continue.

'And the staff who helped her set up, they would have had access to the plans. None of it was a secret. We were just doing the normal set up for the job.'

So that was fairly open then. Anyone could have known. No real help there.

'I'll need names for all of the staff too. And contact details.'

'You might have to ask Kate who specifically knew, but I'll give you a list of everyone who worked on the night.'

'Was it a menu service? Or was this meal one of those where person one has the fish and person two, the chicken?'

'It was our conference special: alternate meals, for every table. Forty dollars a head – though the conference organisers tried to talk me down. I don't know where they thought they'd get a meal this good for cheaper!'

That made Nate stop and think. He'd been to dinners like that – wedding receptions and things where the meals were served alternately. Everyone always got served the meal that they didn't want. There was always a lot of swapping going on – especially when the table knew each other well. But it could have happened here too. What if the meals had been swapped? What if the professor had decided he didn't want the chicken and had swapped it for the steak? What if the poison (whatever it was) had been intended for someone else?

'So was Professor Conneally eating the meal that he was served? Or did he swap his meal for someone else's?'

The manager didn't know the answer to that question and now that he could see where the investigation was headed he started to look intensely nervous. He rubbed his hands on his trousers, and pulled the hanky out of his pocket to give his round glasses an extra clean. Nate could see a muscle twitching just below his right eye.

'You're not suggesting – you think this has something to do with the food?'

'We are investigating every possibility. That's all.'

Edwards wiped his brow. 'Look,' he said urgently, 'this doesn't have to get out, does it? I mean, it's just not good for a restaurant's reputation to be known for poisoning its customers. I hate to think ...'

'Mr Edwards.' Nate became as solemn and officious as he could (and I know just how solemn and officious he can be), 'I am asking questions for the coroner's report. That's all. The coroner needs to know what happened that night. Now, can you tell me, were there any staff put on for the occasion? New staff? What was the staffing interview and background check process like?'

'Well, yes, it was a big deal this dinner, a large crowd. You always get good alcohol sales from things like this, even when the organisers keep the food expenses as minimal as possible. We had a couple of extra wait staff put on for the night. We just asked our staff who they knew that could do the job. Everyone knows everyone around here, you know how it is. We just asked if anyone knew of experienced wait staff that could help out.'

'So no background checks at all then.'

'Ah,' Edwards rubbed his hand over his forehead. He was clearly trying to find some way to duck responsibility for this decision that had seemed the easiest way to go at the time and had turned out to be so ill-advised. 'I'll make sure you know who the new people were when I write my list.'

Nate cut him a break, 'That will be very helpful, thank you. I need to talk to all of them. Anyone here today that was on that night?'

'Yes, yes of course. We have chef here, and a couple of staff. I'm happy for you to talk to anyone. We're not that busy, it will be fine.'

Almost bowing, Edwards had led Nate to the kitchens, all the pride had dripped out of him now that he realised the threat to his restaurant's reputation. Nate didn't want to ruin the business, but he needed to know the truth, and having the manager behind him would make questioning the staff easier.

He started with the chef, Anton Mossier.

Mossier was quite upset that anyone could blame him. His food was always good, his staff, always trustworthy. He didn't let anyone choose his staff except himself, Monsieur Edwards knew that. The kitchen was sacrosanct. All his staff had worked for him for years. He knew their families, they were a family. How dare any measly detective even try to insinuate that one of them could be involved in doing anyone harm. Food was about nourishment, nurture and an artistic experience. Not death and destruction. Never.

He would concede to give Nate the names and numbers of his staff that might be able to say something they had noticed out of the ordinary. But Nate could be sure, if he talked to them, he would see, they had done nothing wrong. Nothing!

That was a full on interview, but it gave the impression that the chef ran a tight ship. He would have noticed something going on in his kitchen and he would have spoken up about it straight away.

The kitchen staff that were around for the morning shift were quick to back up the chef.

'Chef is on our backs all the time. You have to be gold to get a job here – he doesn't just put a random on for the night.'

'He's everywhere in the kitchen. Once I tried to vac the meat, you know, to tenderise it, I nearly lost my job. We do what he tells us – he notices everything.'

Jan piped up, 'I could have told you that. The reputation of The Bay is excellent in food circles.'

Nate threw his hands in the air. 'Next time I'll just ask you to solve it then,' he said, and when Jan laughed and shook her head he continued with his story.

Nate pocketed the list of the off duty kitchen staff to chat to later and turned his attention to the wait staff. Edwards had called in the events manager, Kate, to help with the questioning. Kate was all attention, having been worded up by Edwards to give her full cooperation. She sat at a table with Nate near the front door of the restaurant where they could see the whole room, she made sure they were given coffee and she pulled out her diary with notes from the night so that she could get all the answers correct. Nate wondered whether she was more than just events manager – she was so much more on top of the situation than Edwards. He wondered if the restaurant would be successful without her input. But that really had nothing to do with the situation at hand. He focussed again on imagining the evening as it occurred.

'Yes, the professor was right there on the VIP table and his wife beside him. They were having a good night, really enjoying the evening. It's so unbelievable what happened.'

'Did the Professor swap meals with anyone? Who was sitting on his other side?'

'I think it was, let me check my table plan, yes, it was the lady professor from the USA. Professor Starly." There was another name for Nate's list, "I was watching the table from my position near the door here – I was supervising everything, making sure the staff were doing their job. I love watching people enjoy the meal here. They usually have a great time and it's fun to watch. I'm a real people watcher, you know? I usually expect husband and wife to swap meals – it happens all the time – or they swap half way through, you know, but not the Conneallys. He was too busy eating drinking and talking. He was one of the loudest on the table. So full of life ...' she shook her head sadly.

'Do you have a list of your wait staff? Can you talk me through it?'

'Sure, well the regulars were there – Charlie, Eliza, Yoriko, they are all the normal evening wait staff – they've worked here for years, most of them are uni students, Eliza's not, but the rest are. Then there was Noah and Sally – we put them on for the night. Charlie is finishing up his uni studies soon and he's thinking of leaving us when he gets a teaching position so I was actually giving Noah and Sally a chance to show us what they could do. Sally in particular was a great girl but she's just not reliable, it's such a shame, I would have recommended her to Malcolm for a regular position. I know she needed the work.'

'In what way is she not reliable?' Nate asked.

'Well, as I said, she was great on the night, she called the ambulance and looked after everyone she could once the accident happened but you know, afterwards, she seemed pretty shaken up. I have tried to call her to see how she is, and, incidentally, to offer her a position here, but she hasn't answered her phone. I have left a few messages but she hasn't replied. Such a shame! You know, sometimes they seem great but then –'

'Do you have an address for her?' Nate interrupted.

'Sure – here it is. And here's her number, but like I said, not answering.'

Something was definitely strange there. Nate put a star next to Sally's name and went on with the rest of the interview. Once he'd got all the names and numbers of staff to interview later, and a complete view of the night from all the staff who were present, he decided to wrap it up and head back to his office.

Back at his office, Nate knew that he would need to interview all the remaining staff from the restaurant, and a few more conference delegates, and that meant he needed to get started. And that meant giving a contact list to Beverly, the secretary, and asking her to make the phone calls inviting people to the station. And you have no idea how much Nate liked telling us about this part.

Beverly is the bane of Nate's existence. She, he tells us, is the hardest part of his job – she's tougher than the toughest criminals he's had to interview. And he hated having to ask her to do anything.

Yes, it was her job to contact the people on his list. In fact, he never asked her to do anything that wasn't part of her job – he wouldn't dare! And it wasn't that she didn't work hard, she just seemed to have an aversion to doing anything he asked. He knew that he would be barked at as soon as he placed his request.

Anyway, it had to be done. He needed to be interviewing and sorting and working on the case. She needed to be making the phone calls. He took a deep breath and headed to her desk.

'Beverly, can you –'

'Hang on.' she barked, holding up one hand in a stop sign and then turning back to the computer.

Nate waited a few minutes. 'I really need –'

'Stop, wait!'

Nate waited a few more minutes. Beverly stared at her screen, it looked like she might be filling in a form. She was clicking her mouse incredibly slowly, typing in a few letters at a time. Nate wondered what she was doing but he knew that if he manoeuvred himself to see the screen he would, in Beverly's eyes, be committing a crime worse than murder.

He waited.

Eventually she stopped and looked up, 'What do you want?' The clipped syllables were forced out.

'Could you please bring these people in to the station for an interview?'

'No.'

'What?'

'You haven't given me a print out of your calendar. How can I make interview times without knowing when you're free?'

'Can't you look it up online?' As far as Nate knew, all their calendars were online for a reason, and the reason was that Beverly could look them up and use them to make interview times.

'Didn't you see the email last week? No interview requests without a print out of the calendar for that week. That's the way it's done. Come back when you've got it.'

And that's the way things went with Beverly.

Nate headed back to his office to print out his schedule for the week, a broken man. He usually got on well with office people, talked to them like human beings, gave them gifts and made them coffee. They usually warmed to him and gave him special treatment. But none of his normal tricks had worked with Beverly.

After he'd given her the list and the print out of his schedule, he opened his notebook to Sally's name and number. She seemed to be the strongest lead yet. He would try ringing her himself. If he was honest, the fact that she wasn't answering the phone for the restaurant manager made him reluctant to give her number to Beverly anyway. She would try, put Sally on the bottom of the list and not try again for days. He felt this one was important somehow. He tried the number.

'Hi, you've reached Sally. I'm not here right now but you can leave a message after the beep.'

The chirpy voice recording had come instantly – no ringing at all. That meant the phone was turned off. And what did 'I'm not here' mean? It was a mobile phone number –

here is everywhere you're holding the phone. But that was irrelevant. The meaninglessness of her message bank recording had nothing to do with the case.

He looked through the evidence again. What did he have against Sally? What did he know about her? She was new to the restaurant, but so was Dan. She seemed to have cared a lot when the guy died, which didn't make sense if she was the murderer. All that he had, really, was the emotional state that she was in afterwards (which was not really that strange) and the fact that she wasn't answering her phone.

He tried the phone again. 'Hi, you've reached –' he hung up.

So no real evidence of any wrong doing, but a really strong gut feeling that he was on the right track. Well, he trusted his gut, it was worth following.

He called the crime car and gave them Sally's address. He would see what happened when they brought her in.

Nate got the call. The crime car had picked up Sally at home without much trouble at all and she was waiting for him in the interview room. Well, this was where he found out whether his gut was spot-on this time or whether he had a lot more work to do. He grabbed his notes and headed down the corridor.

As he opened the door a sweet, fragile blonde girl in her late twenties looked up at him from her seat at the table.

'Oh, that's who she was,' I said.

'Who she was?'

'I saw Joshua with her at the conference. During Brasindon's talk. Joshua brought her into the lecture theatre and pointed out someone to her – it must have been Conneally. I wondered what that was about. He must have been setting things up then. Wow.'

'Wow, if only you could have stepped in then,' said Jan. 'You could have stopped a murder.'

'There was no way of knowing,' Nate said. 'Some things are just too well hidden.'

We all agreed and let him get on with his story.

Sally sat slumped at the interview table. She didn't look like she'd been sleeping much, and was obviously upset, but she didn't look like a bad person. But then, life's so much more complicated than that. The world isn't divided into 'bad' and 'good' people. In fact, was there ever a truly good person? Being a good person took a lot more effort than people seemed to think.

'Sally Brelow?'

'Yes.'

'My name is Detective Nathan Fitzgerald, I'm here to ask you a few questions about Professor Conneally.'

Sally started visibly shaking and unsuccessfully tried to hold back her tears as Nate walked in and sat down. He gave a curt nod to the police woman sitting at the table and prepared himself for the questioning.

Nate tried to balance the feelings of success (his gut was definitely right about something) and sympathy (the young girl was a wreck) that were rising in him. He wondered exactly what she had to do with this situation.

He'd had a chat with the crime car guys on the way down to the interview room. They told him that Sally's place of residence was a small unit in the slightly poorer end of town. But she (and whoever else lived there) took care of it – it seemed quite comfortably furnished. A couple of couches and a coffee table sat in front of the large screen TV in the corner. There was a large collection of DVDs on shelving on one wall and they could see some console gaming gear stacked up nearby. There were no books to be seen anywhere – it looked like entertainment was more important to this household than education. They said that there was evidence of a male occupant too-large shoes by the door and a couple of bicycles around the side of the house.

But there was no evidence of smoking or drug taking, the house was well looked after – clean and tidy. There was even a vase of fresh flowers on the front hall table. There was newish furniture and nice blinds on the windows.

It wasn't a dysfunctional household. No evidence of drugs, no need for money, so what was the motivation? Why on earth had this crime been committed? Had it been committed by Sally at all?

'Sally, you were one of the wait staff at the conference dinner held at 'The Bay' last week?'

'Yes.'

'Did you serve Prof Conneally?'

'Yes.'

Nate got tired of the monosyllabic replies. Maybe she was just holding herself together but holding it in was not going to solve this case. If it had to be tears, it had to be tears.

'Listen, I can sit here for as long as it takes. It is obvious to me that you have something to tell me that will help me know why this guy was murdered, its obvious that something is bothering you. I'll wait. You can let me know in your own good time.'

The tears started in earnest then. The 'M' word had a huge effect. Nate waited as the sobs wracked her body. It was like she had been holding her emotion in for days and he had turned the relief valve. He felt for her but at the same time he knew now he was definitely on to something. Finally, the fountain dried up and hiccupping and sniffing, Sally opened up.

'I didn't intend this to happen. It wasn't what I thought would happen. I just thought he would be sick, not that he would die! Not die!'

'How about you start from the beginning.'

'The beginning? I don't really know the beginning. Josh knows. I only know a bit.'

'Who is Josh?'

'You mean, you think it's all me? All my fault?' the valve was open again, the tears flowing and a look of terror on her face, 'It was Josh, it was all Josh, I only ... I didn't know!'

'Ok, ok,' Nate calmed her down. He said that he really wished that Jan could have been there to help out.

The assigned police woman was just sitting there – fulfilling her duty of being present in body but she was not going to get involved, apparently. Nate was pretty much on his own.

'Ok, have a drink, calm yourself down, and tell me about this Josh. It's going to be ok, just let me know your story. Start from the point where you came in.'

'Whatever that meant,' Nate said. 'I was firing arrows in the dark. I really hoped I'd get some clarity, and soon.'

Sally made a valiant effort to pull herself together. She blew her nose, had a sip of water and stared at the desk for a few minutes before taking a deep breath and telling her story.

'I met Josh, Joshua Hume, that is, a few years ago. Oh gosh, maybe eight years? Maybe longer. No, it was our seven year anniversary last year – we must have met eight or nine years ago. He was pretty down – he had just been kicked out of uni for something that wasn't his fault. I mean, if your professor tells you to do something, you do it, right? I mean, he just did what he was told. But the professor got off scot-free and he got all the losses. We would spend hours talking, we really got along well, and I guess that the uni situation was something we talked about a lot. I really felt for him. I wanted to make him feel better.'

'Do you know anything about what went wrong at the university?'

'No, he never told me the story. He said it was too complicated and I wouldn't understand. He just told me how he felt about it and, you know, the general unfairness of it all.'

Nate wondered what Jan would have said if he'd tried to fob her off with the same excuse. He reckoned he wouldn't have heard the last of it for years.

'So you've been together for seven years?'

'Yep, we hooked up together pretty much straight away, he's been the best boyfriend I've ever had but it's been obvious to me that this whole thing has been eating away at him all the time – just in the background, you know.'

'The being kicked out of uni thing?'

'Yeah, it wasn't his fault, he said. It was the professor's fault. But he never suffered anything and Josh lost everything. So when the professor was actually in town for this conference thingy and Josh told me he wanted to do something to make him suffer, well, I thought, why not? I got a position as waitress at the conference dinner and made sure I was assigned to the VIP table. It wasn't hard, I know a lot of people and I'm good at serving.'

'You wanted to make him suffer?'

'Only a little bit.'

'How do you suffer a little bit?' asked Susannah.

'Just to get some of what should have come to him before. Josh had given me some stuff to put on his food. He told me that it would make him pretty sick. Josh told me that when something happened I needed to be there to clear the food away and dispose of it so that no-one could link the sickness to anyone. I thought it was about time that the professor suffered for what he did. I was happy to help Josh out. I mean Josh had suffered! He had suffered for years. Never being able to get a proper uni position. His career had been taken away. It affected his whole life.'

'Right, so you had some "stuff" – what sort of stuff?'

'It was just some powder. I put it on the food. It was just meant to make him sick. But then ...' Sally faltered, 'He was never meant to die! That was never meant to happen. I'm sure that wasn't what Josh meant to happen. When I saw him fall over I just, I hoped that it wasn't my fault, I never set out to kill anyone! He was just supposed to get sick, that's all. Just be sick for a couple of days. It wasn't me that made him die. Was it? I'm sure he was just sick from something else ...'

Sally's voice trailed away as the full force of what she had done closed in on her again. Nate could see that when she thought about Joshua, she could almost make herself believe that what she had done was for the good – a righteous act of vengeance on behalf of an injured person. But once her thoughts turned back to the professor, she realised that she didn't have the authority to take anyone's life.

And while Joshua's situation was pitiable, it did not mean that any of the actions taken were acceptable. Not even the thought of making the professor sick. Revenge just doesn't work, Nate thought, you just have to let it go. For your own sake.

Sally was staring at the table, tearing at one fingernail with her teeth, tears dripping down her face. Nate asked her where he would find Joshua.

Sally looked up at him, totally broken.

'You can't. Don't tell him I told you,' she whispered, 'He would never forgive me.'

'Where do I find him, Sally?' Nate spoke in a firmer voice and Sally responded to authority the way he guessed she always had.

'He's at the university. He works in the Chemistry Department.'

And that's when Nate had decided that I was in trouble. He had remembered Jan telling him that I was working there and he thought about my hair-brained ideas about who committed this murder and my habit of blurting it out to anyone listening – or at least that's what he figured. He felt he had to get to the university immediately, before something went horribly wrong.

'And that's why I came running in.'

'And found that my "hair-brained" ideas were just peachy, thank you very much!'

'I guess so, in the end they were, anyway.'

Now that the story was all told, Susannah, Trudy, and the two students had to head back to the university. We waved them goodbye and I stayed to help Jan and Nate clear off the table.

I had to be honest. 'Nate, it looks like you could have solved this whole thing without me.'

'I'm not sure, your hunch was what got me started.'

Jan asked, 'are you two going to go into partnership now? You could be a great crime fighting team.'

I was considering the question with a smile but Nate was much more certain.

'No,' he stated with great finality and we exploded with laughter.

I agreed. 'I just happened to be in the right place at the right time, with the right amount of information. I couldn't have figured anything out without the knowledge I got from doing the chemical analysis. I'm sure I'll never be in the same situation again.'

'So do you still think you'll work towards a job in academia?' Jan asked.

'I'm beginning to wonder, I just don't know. It's really thrown me that Joshua could get it so out of proportion – that he could think that being an academic was that important. I don't think it's worth killing for.'

'Good, good,' said Nate, stacking the plates in a pile.

'And when you look at Brasindon, he was just so grumpy. He'd given his whole life for research – nothing else mattered – he couldn't even have a fun conversation, let alone a hobby. He lived for the job but he was miserable. I don't want to end up like that.'

'You sure don't,' that was from Jan. I cleared off a few more mugs and took them into the kitchen. And Jan wiped down the table.

'And then Conneally, it looked like he was starting to get the balance right. But how much of his life had he dedicated to the work? And his poor wife, she would have had to put up with the long hours, she was just as dedicated as he was. But then it all came to nothing in the end. His life was just taken away, just like that. It could happen to anyone – a car accident, or cancer, and then it's all gone.'

'This is getting morbid, what are you trying to say?'

'I guess I'm thinking, I want a job, but I'm not sure if I want a job that takes all of your life away. Maybe I'm just not passionate enough about the science, but I want a chance to live a bit too. How much time have I spent in the lab that I wish I could just get back and spend with my mum? Do I want to lose you guys and the community here just so I can do some more science, and get the title 'professor'? I don't know. I think I'm going to have to think on it a bit more.'

'Well, I'm glad. If that means you're with us for a little longer, that's a good thing in my book,' said Jan.

'Yep I'll be staying at least a little bit longer. There's the beach to walk on, the cottage to renovate, and many more coffees to enjoy right here. And I hear Susannah needs a new lab technician ...'

The End.

I hope you enjoyed this story. If you did, please could you leave a review on your favourite vendor website.

Come over to www.rjamos.com and sign up to my newsletter to hear all my news and to find out when the next book is coming out. I'd love to see you there!

Thank you!

Acknowledgements

To my St Clement's family, to have a church family like you is an amazing privilege. Thank you so much for your support of my life journey all the way through. It's so great to go to church and be reminded of what is really important (hint: it's not this book).

To Sandessa, thanks for the friendship first and foremost, and for the technical help as well. Mice and mouse-related research is beyond me and you have saved me from much embarrassment.

To Jules, thanks for the information about the police department. Good to have a friend 'on the inside' (grin).

To Megan, your encouragement and critical help have been essential for both this book and the beginning of my writing journey. You've been my cheer squad from the very beginning. Looking forward to seeing your books in print too.

To Ree and Ray, thank you for making time in your busy family madness to read the novel and give me feedback. I really appreciate your friendship and support.

To Ruth and Keith, I so hope that my journey encourages you on yours. If I can do this, you most definitely can. Thanks for the reading, the many conversations between yourselves, and the roast dinner that softened the feedback that I so appreciated even if it was a little hard to hear.

To Wendee, thank you for your invaluable encouragement and advice. It's been more than helpful to look at the slopes of Everest and see someone a little (or a lot) further on who can show me what to do and how.

To Sheelagh, I can't thank you enough for your expert editing that came with a helpful dose of encouragement. I so needed both.

To my colleagues in the Discipline of Chemistry at UTAS who sat and brainstormed methods of chemistry-related murder over the morning tea table and would then greet me with 'Ruth, I've thought of a new way for you to kill someone' in the hallways, thank you. I hope to make use of many of your suggestions in future novels and you will be glad to hear that the police have not come after me yet.

Mum and Dad, you read the book when no one else was reading it, and you read it more than once.

Your support over the ups and downs has been incredible and I want to thank you so much for instilling in me a love of reading. I will never forget our times together as a family with Dad reading to us. Even if the tears over the book made us look a little strange on family picnics in the park!

Jess and Caleb, you guys rock. Caleb, your little words of encouragement when I felt like everyone else thought I was mad, they helped me keep going. Jess, thank you for believing in me and being so excited when the parcel containing the manuscript turned up at your house.

Moz. What can I say. You are just amazing. Everyone else only has to put up with me on occasion but you have to put up with me every single day. You know more of the elation and disappointment than anyone and you have been so incredibly supportive of this venture. Thank you. I love you.

Other books by R. J. Amos

Deadly Misdirection (Book 2 in the Deadly Miss series)
Deadly Miscalculation (Book 3 in the Deadly Miss series)

Small Town Trouble
Challenge Accepted – A 30-day Short Story Project
The Universe is a Small Place

Find out more at rjamos.com